DREAM
QUARTET

June Ballantyne
Emery Dawn Marcinkoski

tellwell

Tellwell Talent
www.tellwell.ca

ISBN
978-0-2288-6036-5 (Hardcover)
978-0-2288-6035-8 (Paperback)
978-0-2288-6037-2 (eBook)

Table of Contents

Introduction

It started about six months ago when I had a dream; normally dreams are forgotten by the morning, but this one stayed in my head during the day. The next night I had the same dream, but more was added to it, and again it stayed with me during the day. This continued for a number of nights until one night there was an ending to the dream; the next morning I remembered the whole thing, so I went to my desktop and wrote it down.

One Saturday I was talking with my brother Roger in England and he suggested I send it to him to read, which I did, and he edited it. You see it was about Gypsies in England, but I had mentioned chipmunks and skunks and they are not found in England.

Within a week of the first dream I had a second dream, totally different to the first but it happened the same way; pieces were added each night till again this dream came to an end and so I typed it up. This one was much shorter. Roger and I kept it between us; it was our fun secret.

There were no more dreams, but one day I drove down to the Kin beach with my coffee and book, intending to spend a couple of hours reading, but when I looked at the pages I couldn't read the words because sentences kept getting in my way, running across the page. I shook my head but I just couldn't read, so I realized I had to go home and I sat at my desktop and started to type what was coming into my head; I was not making this story up personally, it was just coming to me so fast that I had to type fast, and after typing over five thousand words it was finished; I read it over and it had such a cute ending. However, the next day I got this feeling to get back to my desktop, and the story continued with a different twist, and this one did finish, another three thousand words later. At this point I was feeling concerned, because something was taking over my head and I wasn't sure why. Again I put this in the mail to Roger. I think talking to Roger about it kept my sanity intact.

Then I had to type again, but I don't remember sitting down to type. This one was different, I was feeling sad; I don't remember why now, but sometimes I get the blues. It included some of my own thoughts. Once again it just came and I had to type it down. I am not a writer, I do not have that imagination or ability, it just happened. The dreams stopped, and the writing stopped, and I don't believe it will return. So why did it happen?

Synopses

The Steps of St. Paul's Cathedral: A young girl heads to London to start her career working in the government offices, however an encounter with a young man takes her on a completely new path, to learn about the Gypsy lifestyle and face incredible experiences . . . a far greater challenge than her secure office work would be.

Meeting Miss Juliet: You never know where you might meet your greatest love, and what mysteries it might lead you to.

The Scavenger Hunt, Part 1 and 2: Friends with inexhaustible funds can find so many more ways to make holidays exciting and get into mischief. With trustworthy family members to back you up, there is so much fun you can have on holiday, and no telling what it might lead to.

Grandmother's Wish: Holiday plans may change, and strange things may happen, but is someone overseeing it all?

THE STEPS OF ST. PAUL'S CATHEDRAL

CHAPTER 1

Lunch break at last! It had been a crazy morning with the courthouse requesting documents, and our staff running around getting them copies shipped over to Courtroom Five. I picked up my lunch bag and headed for the elevators with the other girls. Down on the ground we separated and I headed to my favorite spot—the steps of St. Paul's Cathedral. Not very far to walk, I headed up the steps to the far right, and sat leaning against the column, opening my sandwich and my thermos of coffee.

The entrance to the cathedral was busy with tourists wandering in and out, many joining me on the step to take their lunch break. It was a clear day, not too sunny, but noisy with the chatter of adults and the laughter of all the children. Sometimes I liked the noise, other times I liked to sit in the early morning in silence.

I liked to people-watch, and eventually found my eyes on a young man on the lower steps also watching the crowd. He was not dressed as a tourist, more like the Gypsies I had seen in the countryside near home. His eyes seemed to pick one group after another, and so I kept my eyes on him; he was keenly watching the younger people. I thought that he was probably a pickpocket, watching for his next victim. Then he realized that I was watching him, so I kept my eyes on him in hopes of putting him off his task. Instead, he continued to look at me, and soon I had to look away.

Lunch was coming to an end, I packed up my thermos, went down the steps and turned to the right, walking past the young man and dropping my garbage in a bin hidden in the bushes.

I walked around the side of the cathedral heading back to work, when I realized the young man was following me. Taking the strap of my purse, I put it over my head, with the purse tucked under my arm. He was getting closer, so I took a nearby street and walked fast, until I came to a small convenience store where I stepped inside. The young man followed me in, and without looking at me, he walked to the back of the store and into the back rooms. I quickly turned and walked outside the store again and turned to my left, where he stepped out from the alley in front of me.

I tried not to show that I was afraid, saying "You're following me, if you don't go away I will scream for help." He half smiled at me and said that yes, he was following me, and that he wanted to talk with me. I told him that he couldn't because I was going to work and he was making me late.

Stepping back, he apologized, and I looked around and realized I was lost. He grinned, saying that he could get me back to my workplace on time, on the condition that I met him after work for a talk. I hated to do it, but I had to agree, and he dragged me by the hand, through the back alleys of London at a fast pace, and I was soon at the side entrance to the government building where I worked.

We worked tirelessly all day putting together the documents and requirements for the busy courtrooms that we serviced, and today was a particularly difficult day and no one left when five o'clock came. I stayed until 6:45 p.m. and when I left the building, I saw the young man across the road and lean against the far building.

He started to walk down the road, expecting me to follow. I hesitated, then followed him. Catching up, and in my annoyed fashion, I asked him where we were going. He didn't speak so I stopped and turned around, but he quickly took hold of my arm, pulled me around, and said his name was Tom and that we had to walk quickly.

We walked in silence, heading for the docks—not a nice neighborhood for me to go to. He pulled me close to him, and we headed to some of the big warehouses with huge hanger doors, where Tom opened a regular door to the left.

We entered and, although it was poorly lit, I saw six Romani wagons around the outer wall; I could not see the horses that pulled the wagons. In the center of the building were rugs, blankets, and stools, with logs to sit on. There were at least a dozen adults sitting around, smoking pipes and cigars; the air was thick with the smoke.

A girl stepped from the back of one of the wagons. She came slowly, looking at Tom, then at me, and as she got closer I felt uncomfortable in my stomach; she looked much like me; she had longer, black hair, and it was tied with different ribbons, but her face was very like my face, and she was about my size. She stood still for some time studying me, and glancing back and forth between me and Tom, and suddenly she ran over to Tom and started pounding him on his chest, kicking at him, and yelling at him, "Why did you have to bring her here, you're cruel to do this to me, take her away and never bring her back." She continued to beat at him, and yell abuse, and I was just so confused. Tom kept saying that he was sorry, that he had not meant to hurt her, he just thought that I should know. But know what?

All the adults that had been seated were now standing, and they threw dark looks towards Tom and me. One man came over and said, "Get her out of here before trouble erupts." Tom grabbed my hand and took me over to the left corner of the building where there was a door that led into a fenced yard for the horses. He lifted me up onto the bare back of one of the horses and jumped up behind me. We left in silence and he took me back to my road where I lived, stopping at the entrance. He lifted me down, saying that he was sorry and that he would get in touch with me soon to explain.

The weekend came and I did not hear from Tom, joining my girlfriends on a shopping spree along Oxford Street, and later we went to the park and played softball, laying on the grass eating snacks and taking cold drinks. I considered trying to find the warehouse, but the thought of walking down by the docks alone and vulnerable stopped me from going.

Monday came and I decided to head to work early to take a morning rest on the steps of St Paul's Cathedral. It was a crisp morning, and I took a cushion to sit on, loving the peace and quiet, except for the birds twittering their greetings to the visitors as their part of London life. I was about to head to work, when I heard the clatter of horses and wagons approaching, so I stepped back into the shade of the foliage. Two wagons appeared, with men, women and children walking alongside the wagons, it looked like they were leaving the city. I was going to step down and find out whether they were all leaving, when a hand came around my waist and another hand over my mouth. Tom whispered in my ear to not make a fuss.

We both watched the wagons and families pass by and I turned to Tom with so many questions. He looked sad and explained to me that, because he had taken me to their winter camp, the elders had decided to move out to their summer quarters a month early. He said they would be travelling throughout the countryside for a couple of months, but that they would settle into summer quarters by the month of May, and he gave me a piece of paper with the address where I could find them. He told me that the other four wagons had left earlier that morning, so he had to run and catch up with the last wagon. He then touched my shoulder gently, before running off.

CHAPTER 2

I returned to my work that morning with the start of an idea, and later contacted payroll and asked if, instead of being paid for my overtime on payroll, could I save the hours up and add them to my vacation time. There was no problem with that, which set in motion my planning for the summer.

The months went by quickly, my mind was filled with excitement at what I would find and do during my summer vacation. I did a little shopping, buying a good sleeping bag and pillow, some warm PJ's, and easy-to-wash shirts and shorts.

Time flew by, the beginning of May arrived, and I booked my train ticket and completed my packing into one rather large travel backpack. I had already phoned my parents, letting them know that I was taking a holiday with friends; I felt guilty because this was my first time choosing to take my holiday away from home.

Heading for the train station, I soon found myself in a carriage with five grammar-school students who were on holiday together; the carriage was filled with chatter and laughter, and occasionally singing. We shared the lunches we had brought along and rested a short while after eating. My station arrived and I left the happy crowd to continue their journey.

Stepping out into a small station alone, I went inside and asked about a bus, showing the porter the paper with my final destination. The attendant said he was sorry but the bus had just left; another would not be ready for an hour. That was OK, I sat on the wooden bench for a while, then went outside and climbed the hill behind the station and was able to look out over the rail lines to fields with cows, beautiful rock walls and hedges separating fields—such peaceful settings. Time went quickly and I could see a bus coming along the lane so I skipped my way back to the station.

Once on the bus I showed the conductor the address to where I was headed, he gave me a nice smile saying, "Sit back, it's a little ways away." It was a beautiful drive, sometimes offering views across fields, other times hedges blocked the view but there were so many spring flowers to see, and occasionally the trees on either side blocked all views as they were so tall and met above us over the road.

The bus slowed and stopped at the side of the road, and the driver called me forward. He pointed to a gate on the right saying, "Go through the gate and it's just a short walk till you see the main house. Don't go up to the manor, but as soon as you see it, turn to the right and go across the fields. Keeping the trees to your right follow them down to the lake, you will find the encampment there." Then he asked me if I had gum boots, which I did. He told me to put them on before I got off the bus. I thanked him for his advice and waved to him as I went through the gate.

I had only been walking about five minutes when the manor house came into view, it was a three-storey building, with a chimney on the peeked roof, lots of windows, and a beautiful rock wall all round. I turned and cut across the field, following the tree line on a gentle slope. Going down the fields I could see the lake up ahead, and a number of wagons. Before I reached the wagons Tom came out of the trees behind me and made me jump; he was laughing and soon I was laughing with him. As we got closer I realized that there were far more than the six wagons that were at the docks. Tom explained that they had all separated to small groups travelling to places to rest for wintertime, and that here was the full tribe, with over forty wagons of different sizes and ages, and a couple of very modern petrol driven motor homes. They were not set in a circle, but along both sides of a Roman road, which was like cobblestones set into the soil, and was very old—I knew this from school.

Tom threw my gear into the back of a wagon, and we walked along the road talking, well he was talking mostly, telling about the people and the way they lived, that there were many large families going back generations, and all travelling together. He pointed to a large wooden building and let me know that I could have a shower and wash my clothes there, and that there were a number of other facilities along the road. The land was part of the manor house grounds, however the fields used by the wagons and horses were left to the families in a will.

We returned along the road and stopped at a large area of mats with stools, logs and deck chairs for us to sit down, and Tom introduced me to his aunts and uncles and cousins; all looked at me with curiosity. There were two large pots hanging over fires, on crossed iron stands, and a table set close to the wagon with huge loaves of fresh bread and piles of wooden bowls. Tom took one of the bowls, ladled the stew into it, and told me to pull off a piece of bread and sit down, then he gave me the bowl. He joined me, and everyone took their bowls of stew and sat around eating quietly.

It was now dark and I was tired after a long travel day. Tom said it was still too damp to sleep outside so he stepped up into the wagon and set my sleeping bag out, and told me to do whatever I wanted and get myself to bed. I had the uncomfortable feeling that this was Tom's wagon, and hesitated before making any move. One of the men in the circle looked at me with a serious face, saying that it was Tom's wagon and that he would not dare take one move out of place, that he knew the consequences, and the voices around and nods by some of them confirmed this as Tom looked away from me. I climbed up into the wagon and settled down into my sleeping bag, snuggling up on the pillow. Tom came in much later and got quietly into his bedding and we slept.

I woke feeling refreshed, Tom was sitting on the steps, he smiled and asked if I would like to go for a walk. I put on a warm sweater and my gum boots and we headed to the woods, which he called a copse. As we entered the sun was shining through the branches, the ground was covered in bluebells; it was a fairy garden. I could hear wild animals moving through the undergrowth, and we sat on a log to wait and see what was wandering around us. There were mice, squirrels, even a fox, and Tom said that one morning he had seen a badger; I would have liked to see a badger.

When ready we returned to the wagon and Tom showed me how to clear up the floor of the wagon ready for the day, and where to put my backpack and clothes.

Breakfast was chunks of bread and cheese and hard-boiled eggs, with huge mugs of tea to warm us inside. I watched the men head out to a field of horses, and I helped with washing the mugs and other dishes. Some of the ladies took up the task of scrubbing out the stew pots, and others got together to make the dough for buns and loaves. Later I helped peel apples and chop them ready for pies, it was a busy day, and really very enjoyable.

In the afternoon one of the ladies suggested I walk over to the paddock where the men were riding horses round a track, going through various paces. Tom was in a far field with a horse on a long rein, going in a circle around Tom, who was teaching him something; I wasn't at that point sure of what. He waved to me but carried on and didn't come over. Some of the boys were down beside the lake fishing, and a number of the children were on the hillside playing; it was such a peaceful moment.

I wandered down the center of the wagons to the far end, and then through the field and up toward another copse. As I arrived at the top of the field, two large St Bernard dogs came bouncing down toward me. I stood still and they jumped up on me licking my arms and face, so I began to play with them. They were very beautiful and kept bouncing to the top of the hill, and shortly I realized we were at the back of the manor house. There was a large concrete patio surrounded by a beautiful stone wall, with three glass tables and umbrellas, the chairs turned upside down on the tables. Behind this patio was a large extension to the manor. The dogs ran through an open gate and across the patio to the open doors, so of course, I followed the dogs.

I stood at the entrance of what appeared to be a beautiful library, staying still for a while. I love books so I just couldn't stop myself from taking a couple of steps into the room. There was a huge old desk, padded chairs, and ladders for reaching the higher bookshelves; the air smelled of leather and old books. There were two pictures on the desk, one of a gray-haired man with a teenage girl, and the other was an older wedding photo. I moved over to the book shelves, the dogs forgotten, and was reading along the titles when a loud voice boomed at me, "What are you doing back here, didn't I tell one of your kind just this morning to get out of my house and stay out, keep your hands off everything here, now get out, next time I will hold you by the scruff of your neck and call for the police." He was huge, with white hair, glaring eyes, and must have been well over six feet tall. I wanted to protest, but as I tried to speak he stepped forward, so I turned to the door and ran. I ran and tumbled all the way down the hill until I felt safe, and stood up to take a breath. What was that all about, that was my first time wandering away from the wagons, and what a temper he had.

CHAPTER 3

That evening, as we sat around eating dinner, I asked Tom if he knew anything about the people in the manor house. He asked me why I wanted to know. I told Tom about my experience, and obviously others had been listening because I heard a comment that sounded like "I said this girl would be trouble." Tom said we should talk later, and we continued quietly with our meal.

After dinner, Tom wandered away, and I stayed in the circle where they were playing music and singing and the children were dancing; it certainly was a fun life.

Tom came back and introduced me to his Uncle Jack, saying that he would be able to answer my questions, his uncle suggested we take a walk into the copse away from little ears. We found a comfy log in the copse; it was so beautiful with the bluebells and cowslips.

Tom's Uncle Jack started by saying, "Lord Thornbush purchased the manor house and moved in with his new wife years back, before the wagons parked by the lake. We used to take the wagons to some fields close to a couple of villages nearby, where the farmers let us have places to park in exchange for us helping on the farms. We had a good life and got on well with many of the people in the villages. This of course was before Tom was born.

Then one day we heard that the lady at the manor had had a baby, but within days she had died from the child's birth. They had a baby girl, and he called her Rose, but the Lord was so sad that he hired a nanny to look after the little girl, and later he arranged for home schooling, so she was a quiet, lonely child, and had few children to play with. When she was sixteen she was sent away to a finishing school, and on her return was considered a sweet girl, she would go into the villages and to the town window-shopping, having a friendly way with all the people that she spoke with.

While wandering through one of the villages, she met Michael Smith, one of the young men from our tribe, and they would eventually spend a lot of time together. Michael had his own reason for trying to keep their relationship quiet, but time went on and they knew they were in love. They first went to Lord Thornbush who lost his temper on the doorstep. Pulling his daughter inside, he took a rifle from behind the door and threatened Michael that if he ever came near his daughter again, he would use the gun on him.

Michael was unable to talk with Lord Thornbush, and he went off by himself. He went back to his family and told them what he wanted to do; now he received a hard lesson from his family, because he knew that a Romani Gypsy was not to marry a non-Gypsy, it would be very hard for her to be accepted into the family, and of course he knew that. However, love overcomes all, and he and Rose made plans of their own."

Jack continued, "Early on a warm sunny morning, Michael moved his wagon out from the rest of his circle and went over to the manor where Rose was waiting with her bags. They piled everything in the back, but as Michael was lifting Rose up front, her father came out and said that if she went with the Gypsy she would never be allowed back. Rose was crying, but she climbed into the wagon, and they left together, going over to the caravan where Michael spoke with his family. He was told that he would have to leave their caravan for the next twelve months, and that, if they survived as a couple, they would be able to come back as a new wagon family joining the caravan.

Michael and Rose were very sad as they left and headed in the direction of Essex where Michael had a number of friends. It was a learning time for both of them, having to get odd jobs on building sites, and jobs on the farm, and Rose learned how to do housework for the farmhouses. They were so very happy and had many friends in the new circle that let them join in their family evenings, and occasional festivities."

It was much cooler, and Jack suggested that we stop for the night, and continue another day. Personally, I could have listened all night, but everyone had to work the next day, and so we went back to sleep.

The following day moved so slowly; inside I was so excited for Jack to continue with the story. Dinner came and everyone spent a little more time talking and dancing, but eventually settled down when Jack nodded his head toward the copse, and Tom joined us.

Once we were settled on the log, with extra blankets, Jack continued telling the story. "A year later Michael and Rose were ready to go home, and they were excited because they had special news to tell their families. They were nearing the railway station on the highway when a huge fully loaded haulage truck crossed the center line and crashed into their wagon, killing the horse instantly and smashing the wagon to pieces. The first attenders were called, and two bodies were taken from the wagon to the morgue in the town. News travels fast, and Michael's uncle and two other men headed to the morgue, they would not let any of the ladies attend. It was a terrible sight and the men had to look at their two loved ones and asked for chairs so that they could sit awhile. One of the nurses on duty that night was from their caravan, and she came and sat with them, holding each of their hands in turn.

They had been sitting for a while when Michael's uncle said Rose was moving, the nurse went over to Rose and was shocked to find that something was moving inside her. She ran for the young doctor on duty, and they agreed; there was a baby alive inside Rose. What would the authorities do with a Gypsy baby? there was some hard talking back and forth with the nurse, doctor and men, but eventually the nurse went and found all that was needed for a cesarean. All was ready and, not telling anyone that it was her first cesarean, the doctor delivered a tiny black-haired baby girl, who was instantly wrapped in a warm, cuddly blanket. While waiting for the afterbirth, another baby appeared, blonde-haired, and very, very tiny, and the doctor said that she probably wouldn't last the night; however she was also wrapped in a warm cuddly blanket, and handed to one of the men.

Now what to do, somehow no one wanted to report the births, so the nurse told the men to take the babies back to one of the wagons. She gave them powdered food and a few necessities, saying she would follow at the end of her shift, then she and the doctor cleared away all the evidence of the operation, and agreed not to mention it again. One of the men had gone to the manor house, but Lord Thornbush had come out with a shotgun, threatening him and telling him to get away or he would shoot.

The nurse arrived at the wagon and they discussed what to do with the babies. The answer was easy for the black-haired baby, because she also had a light olive skin and looked like any member of the caravan; there just happened to be a couple who had two small sons. After contacting them, and just a little more discussion, they were happy to add the pretty little girl to their family. Then what to do with the tiny blonde-haired white-skinned baby, knowing that they could not put this baby with any of the wagons, there would be too many questions.

The baby survived the night and so I decided to wander into a couple of the villages and see what I could come up with. After sitting in a few pubs and coffee shops, I heard a couple of ladies talking about friends who were returning to their village after a year away; they had been farming some distance away and had been newlyweds when they left. I located where the couple were coming from, finding my way to their neighborhood, where they were loading up a trailer with their household goods ready for the trip back to the village.

I made myself welcome and just slipped in helping them to load and get ready for the afternoon journey and asked if I could travel with them in exchange for helping unload at their destination. It turned out to be a very pleasant afternoon, and I had a good feeling about the young couple, and once all of the helpers had left at the new house I asked the couple if I could talk with them. I explained that two of our clan members had died, and that they had a small baby, but, because they were a Gypsy family, we thought the state would not make any priority for this tiny baby. I suggested that, as this couple had moved back to the village, no one would know that it wasn't their baby. They protested at first, but when they were told that the baby would end up being looked after by three very old men, they eventually agreed, and the tiny baby joined them that night.

Months later, after the loss of their young family, the caravan received a visit from a lawyer with documents leaving the fields along the lake and the copse to Michael's family. They had been left in Rose's will; she had been a very wealthy young woman, with money and lands left to her by her mother. Lord Thornbush took it to court, but he lost, and the wagons made a trail down the side of the copse to the fields below, and had been spending some months of the summers there ever since.

Over the years I kept an eye on the little family, they had babies of their own, all boys, and they continued to be loving parents to the little blonde girl. As time went on Tom eventually took over watching out for the little girl, who became a teenager, attended college, and one day left the village. He later found her working in London. That was you."

I realized that I was forgetting to breathe, and my tummy was quite queasy. I took some deep breaths, then Jack made me tuck my head down for a while. What a shock, bringing on such strange feelings. Firstly, I was adopted. Secondly, I had a twin sister. Thirdly, I was not who I thought I was.

Jack suggested we go back for the rest of the evening, and I could take time to think, and once I was ready, he would start to answer my further questions. I felt I was in a fog as we returned to the wagons, and I went straight to bed, not sleeping, nor hearing Tom as he settled for the night.

CHAPTER 4

In the morning I told Tom and Jack that I had to go home to my parents and let them know what I had learned. I had parents and grandparents that I had grown up with. I told Tom that I would only be away three to four days.

Mum and Dad were surprised and happy to see me, and that evening I told them of my discovery. Mum cried and Dad looked sad but I told them that no one could take their place in my life. Dad then told me that it was all true, but I had been their baby from the instant they picked me up.

Dad also told me that there was a connection he had with me that very few knew about, my dad was from a Romani family, his father was Romani, however Mum and Dad didn't consider themselves Romani, having lived in housing all their lives.

I spent four happy days with my parents, wandering the fields and around the village, and they realized that nothing would change between us; they were still my family.

Tom met me at the train station and we took the bus back together. I felt at peace, knowing that my parents were not objecting to me learning about this side of my family.

One afternoon I wandered down the center of the wagons, going slowly, hoping to see my twin. I wandered over to the other copse and she was sitting on a log just inside the trees, looking out over the lake. I asked if I could sit beside her, and she nodded. We were quiet for some time, then she said, "So you know now." I said yes and she admitted that she was afraid of the repercussions my knowing would have on those involved in our birth, and I said that what had happened in the past would stay there. I thought she had been given a pretty name—Violet. We looked alike, at least our features were the same, but she was stunning with her long black hair and olive skin, which had darkened with a lifetime of being out in all weathers. We shared a great deal about our lives growing up, we laughed a lot, and I found my sister to be someone I look forward to getting to know more.

CHAPTER 5

My holiday was coming to an end, what should I do, I didn't want to return to London, but I had to work and earn money to live. Also, if these people let me stay with them, did I want to, could I live the life they lived?

During my final week the weather had really changed, and with it came thunder, lightning, and constant rain. This was really unusual weather and the men had a meeting, one of them advised that they needed to get everyone and everything away from the open ground. We all packed everything into the wagons; they were all hitched up and moved slowly to the copse close to us, they took the wagons close along the bottom edge of the copse, facing a number of wagons, and then clustered the other wagons behind them. Taking ropes, they tied the wagons to each other, and then to the big trees, and they took the horses inside the copse and tied them to trees.

It rained all day and all night. We woke up to the trees on the manor grounds bent to the ground, the roofs from the wash house and the other wooden structures were gone. The wind was howling and we could hardly stand, we were all told to stay close to the wagons, and if necessary to get under them.

I wondered how the Lord was, whether he was safe in his house. Tom decided to make his way up the side of our copse and see if he could get across to the house. He tied himself to trees as he made his way upwards, and we could hear some trees snapping. Suddenly there was a terrific roar, like a train racing at us, and I could see the hillside above the house move, the trees and rocks were crashing down towards the back of the manor, then I saw it coming past the back of the manor, mud, water, trees, and huge rocks, together having destroyed the beautiful patio, taking the furniture, the rock wall, and so much more with it. The roar was so loud; I had never witnessed such a slide in my life.

The Lord came out of the front door, and fell to the ground, he tried to get up to walk, but he was thrown down to the ground again and was trying to crawl. Tom threw ropes with hooks across to some of the bent trees up ahead and was using them to pull himself across to the manor. The Lord was rolling down the hill, pushed by the storm, his foot was caught in the mud, which was pulling him over.

Tom realized that he would be gone soon if he himself couldn't reach him, and so he stood up and threw himself forward. Crashing to the ground and going into a fast roll, he got close to him, and was able to grab at his hand. Tom pushed his feet into the muddy lawn and pulled as hard as he could, he shifted them both out of the mud, and away, managing to get close and tie a rope joining their belts together. The wind was too strong, it was pushing them down the hill at the same time that the mud slide was crashing past the far copse; they just kept tumbling, and Tom yelled at the Lord to try and direct his body to the back of the wash houses.

They worked together, crashing into the back of the wash houses; Tom was dragging them both around the side of the building, away from the slide, and was pulling them both to the entrance; he was choking from exhaustion and dropped his head to the floor, managing to pull them inside in front of a shower. Once he had recovered a little, he looked at the Lord and realized he was unconscious. The roof was missing from the wash house, and so were large parts of the walls, but the tiled showers and plumbing were still standing, and he lay down and put his head on his arms. He knew he couldn't do any more, and listened as the mud slide continued close by and the storm roared itself out.

Tom woke when someone was shaking him and asking him if he was hurt. They helped him up, and two others were looking after the old man who appeared to be in poor shape. They had hitched one of the horses to a small wagon and carried the old man out and headed for the town to the hospital. Everyone was coming out of their shelters, hugging each other and glad to see that no one had been injured. They all walked along the lake to where Tom and the other men were, and were glad to see that the mud slide had stayed to the far side of the lake, entering it at the very far end.

We all looked up the hill, relieved to see that the house was still standing, except that the slide had travelled across the back of the manor taking out the patio, building up three to four feet of mud and rock against the extension to the back of the building.

The following days were a blur of survival as we stayed close to the trees, with the men rebuilding the huts, washrooms and ovens so that food could be cooked. Four of the young men were sent into the nearest village to help where they could. When they got closer they saw the two St. Bernard's crawling out from under the basement area to the side of the house; they eventually made their way to the wagons and settled in quite nicely.

It took a few days until we were able to move the wagons back along the track in front of the lake, and that evening we had a small celebration. Everyone had survived and the horses were well, even if a little skittish still. I had missed my return to work, and eventually phoned them and said that I would not be returning, and I also called my parents to let them know that I was OK and that I would be staying where I was for now.

CHAPTER 6

One lunchtime an ambulance drove up to the house and the Lord was helped inside the manor house. One of the ambulance men with him came down to us and asked if anyone here was able to look after him, and Jack looked at me with a question in his eyes as he spoke; he said that I would go up. When we were alone Jack said that he was sorry, but I was the only "white" person that the old man might accept.

He walked with me to the manor and came inside and spoke to the old man, telling him that I was here to help him, then Jack set to with lighting a fire, pulling the old man's chair closer, with a table beside him.

I had been making tea and when Jack left I pulled up the other chair and made tea for each of us. He didn't say anything, he just kept looking at me. I told him about the damage outside; he was so sad, I suggested that men from the caravan would be able to do most of the work to repair the patio, they could get machinery to help clear away the mud and rock at the back of the house, and they were experienced with construction and road building, and building walls would be easy for them. He nodded but didn't say anything.

I went for a walk around inside, we were in a small lounge and, with the glass doors closed, we were quite snug. There were also much bigger rooms: a dining room, music room, and larger greeting area. I found the kitchen had storage rooms where there were containers of canned fruits, flour, meats, and some vegetables. There was also a small guest room and washroom near to the kitchen.

Returning to the Lord, I asked if he would prefer to sleep on the ground floor until he was stronger. He agreed, so I went back and made up the bed and checked that everything was in order for him to stay there. Then I went to the kitchen and started making a light supper. Jack popped in some time in the afternoon and put more logs on the fire, and peeking into the kitchen he said he would be back in the morning and wished me good night. At that point I felt quite alone and wondered how I would manage the night.

Supper made, I found a lap tray and took the food to the Lord, and took my own to spend time by the fire. He ate a small amount and then closed his eyes. I took the dinner tray away and asked him if he would like to go to bed. He said no, that he just needed to rest his eyes for a while, and then he said that he would like me to tell him what had happened the night of the mud slide.

I did the dishes while he took his rest, and later he asked me to relay the events of that night. I told him that I had not seen everything, but that Tom had told us all what had happened before he himself passed out. He looked at me saying, "In all that storm, all the danger that was roaring around us, he came to find me and came to my rescue, he risked his own life, we could have easily been pulled into the mud and rocks, but he decided to save me," he was shaking his head from side to side and staring into the fire.

Later I helped him to the bedroom and he sat on the bed and said he would manage the rest. I looked in on him later and he was snoring comfortably. Wandering upstairs I found that all the bedrooms were very large, however there was one that covered my needs, and it was a comfortable night's sleep.

In the morning Jack arrived with some baking from the lady's kitchen, and a chunk of cheese for us. I made a pot of tea and thin cheese sandwiches while Jack started a new fire. The Lord asked Jack if he had time to sit a while, and he asked Jack about more of the events of the night of the slide, and how they had survived and what they had been doing since to put life back in order for themselves.

He asked if Jack would help him outside to see the damage around the manor; they found the wheelchair and went out the front door—the back patio being clogged with mud. There had been a huge greenhouse, the metal frame was still standing but all of the glass had gone and there was mud a foot deep throughout. Going around the front of the manor they could see the mud and rocks coming out from the back of the building; it was a devastating sight.

The Lord was taking some deep breaths, Jack touched his shoulder and said that it was not as bad as it looked, that it could all be cleared and repaired. Jack brought him back into the lounge and set him in the chair by the fire. The Lord asked him if he would come back in the evening to talk; Jack went back to the caravan and I got on tidying, dusting, keeping the teapot hot, and preparing little snacks to encourage the Lord to eat. I made a light dinner, but once again the Lord only ate a small amount.

Later that evening Jack returned, and I left them to talk beside the fire. I took a chair outside and enjoyed the late evening sky and closed my eyes for a rest. When Jack came out he told me that he had agreed with the old man on a contract to work on the back of the house. It would mean renting some heavy equipment, but they knew where to get all the machinery, and he said that they would make it as good as new. He smiled at me and wandered back to the caravan.

The Lord said that he was ready for bed and he tried to stand and fell forward, but I did get to him in time to stop the fall, and I helped him to the bedroom and wished him goodnight.

CHAPTER 7

By lunchtime the next day the large equipment had arrived, some of the men from the caravan were using it to push the mud away towards the copse; it was a huge job with the rocks and trees stuck in the mud. They worked for days creating a wall down beside the copse. At the bottom end by the lake, the mud and rocks had already been pushed away from the wash house and the lake. They worked the ground around the back of the manor so that if there was another mud slide, it would go down to the copse, however so much had washed down that I doubted there would ever be another slide.

We settled into a routine in the house, with occasional visits from people at the encampment; we would enjoy conversations, attempting to put the world to rights, and I would read to him each evening. One day he asked me how the mud slide had affected my life, and I told him that I had come to the end of a holiday and was planning to return to London when the slide came. I told him that after the slide I had decided to stay with the caravan and had let my work and parents know what I was doing, saying that I still had to find work soon. The Lord suggested he pay me for my services, but I explained to him that this was something that the elders had said we would do for him, and that no, he was very kind, but I could not ask for any payment.

Later he had a bright light to his eyes and he asked me to take him in to the library. It was lighter back there now that the mud had been taken away from the doors and windows. The Lord looked around and asked me if I knew anything about libraries, and I confirmed that I worked in records and could find my way round a library. He then asked if I would like to catalog his library, that he would pay me, and it would probably take months. I was very excited about the idea and agreed immediately.

He then opened a side door in the hallway, it opened into the greenhouse, and he told me he hadn't used it for years, however he still wanted it repaired, and maybe we could grow some tomatoes this year. I told him that I would ask the elders to see who was most suited for the work, and later that day I walked to the caravan and found one of the ladies and told her of the situation and the work that was expected. They all agreed that Tom was the right person to repair the glass and the inside of the greenhouse and start plantings.

I found Tom working on the wash house and let him know what had been suggested; he grinned and said of course he was the right person, he loved planting and it would give him great pleasure; he came up to see the Lord that evening.

Days later the Lord came into the library where I was working asking me to join him in the lounge and to bring in some tea. The fire was roaring and we settled into the two chairs with our tea. He said that he had some questions to ask me, that they could be personal, but he felt that there was a connection between us that he couldn't understand.

I knew that this question would one day come and suggested that we needed something a little stronger than tea and I went over to the cabinet and poured us drinks. I said that I would take the story backward, that way he would know how I came to be at the encampment. He was always saying he couldn't understand why a white girl would want to stay there for a holiday. I told him how I first met Tom, and how I found myself walking down his field to the encampment, and how I met Jack, and over a few days how Jack had explained the circumstances of my birth, and that I had gone home and confirmed with my parents that it was all true.

The Lord asked me what those circumstances were, and I told him we would both need another drink because they included him. I then told him how Michael and Rose had been sent away by him and Michael's people. That they had spent a year away working on the farms, and Rose had been house cleaning at a farmhouse; he took out his handkerchief at that point and turned his head away.

I continued with a slightly changed story, I didn't think he could handle the actual events concerning the birth of the twins. I told him that Michael and Rose were bringing their newly born babies to the encampment, but they had left them at the hospital and were coming alone first when they were hit by the huge haulage truck and were killed. I told him that Michael's family heard of the accident and had gone to the hospital morgue, where they had been told about the babies. When Jack had tried to approach him to tell him of the babies, he came out with a gun and threatened him never to come back.

I then explained how the decision was made to keep one girl at the encampment with a loving family, and that eventually they found a good white family for me to live with, I said that I had had a happy life with a loving family.

Months had gone by, and the back of the manor had been cleared of any signs of the slide, except for the wall it had created down the side of the copse. There was a beautiful new patio, and a wall with a gate around it. The front was cleared of all debris, and the greenhouse was looking really good with the inside cleaned out and the new glass installed, and Tom was building benches inside. Tom and I had been seeing a lot of each other during those months and had become quite close. When I said that the Lord was well enough for me to leave, Tom said that I couldn't return to his wagon. I was shocked and asked him why; when he just looked at me, I realized why.

CHAPTER 8

One morning I found the courage to ask Jack where Tom's parents were. It was a very sad story. Jack said "When Tom was eleven years old, there was a flu epidemic went through the south of England. Tom and his parents all went down with the flu, Tom recovering quite quickly. However, both his parents had it really bad, and were not able to recover. Tom lost both his parents within two weeks of each other.

Following their funeral Tom went off the rails, he went into the town throwing rocks and smashing many windows. Once in the town he went to the telephone kiosks and pulled out the phones and smashed the glass of the kiosks; then he started to toss the garbage cans into the street. That was when the local police picked him up and called me.

I attended with Tom at the judge's chambers, and explained to them the events of the last month, and that Tom was acting out his pain. His sentence was to either repair or pay for the repair of all the windows that he had smashed. He would have to work to pay for the damage to all the telephone kiosks, and work for the garbage company for a month, that way he would realize how difficult it was for them to clean up his mess.

We returned to the caravan, but later that day I found him packing his clothes in a bag, getting ready to leave; he was still incredibly angry and ready to fight me and anyone who tried to stop him.

With help, I got hold of him and we sat him down in front of one of the wheels of his parents' wagon, and we tied him to the wagon, and left him there. He screamed and yelled at us with words you would not want to hear, we left him there to burn himself out. He continued all that afternoon and evening, and whenever I went near him he would still voice his anger. That night I put a blanket around him, leaving him tied to the wheel. In the morning he was quiet. He ate his breakfast, but I could still see the anger in him, and I kept him tied to the wheel, this time trying to talk some sense into him. By that evening the tears came, and I untied him and took him into my arms, he sobbed his pain away, eventually saying he was sorry.

I worked with him to repair windows, and then he had to find work to pay for the damages. It took him over eight months, I think he felt good, especially once he had finished working for the garbage company. At this point I knew that he had to have some responsibility to keep him occupied. He took over his parents' wagon and repainted it to his liking. I had the idea to get him to take over watching out for you. He had to cycle into the town and village every few days and report back to me. You were his savior in that respect, he had a responsibility that he took seriously." I thanked Jack for sharing with me and felt the compassion for the young man I was learning to care for.

CHAPTER 9

One morning the Lord asked me if my sister Violet would come for a visit, and after breakfast I walked down to the caravan and found her reading a book in the sunshine. She did not like what I asked of her, and turned aside to go into her wagon, when I continued to explain how nice he was now, how he had cried when he heard of the circumstances of our birth and lives, and how we had been separated from him. She gave in and walked up the hill with me.

She didn't want to go inside the manor but sat on the wall outside, and I went in to bring the Lord outside. He asked her questions and she told him about her life with her family and living within the encampment, all her answers showed him that she had been loved and that she was happy.

It wasn't all work and no play; Tom and I enjoyed trips into the town to the market and the cinema; and we were enjoying taking hikes with other young people from the caravan. We surprised Mum and Dad by going for a weekend to see my whole family, and Tom was instantly made "one of the boys." The Lord opened the lawns more to the caravan people, and we would frequently have games for the children while the men prepared BBQs, and the ladies put on incredible spreads of food. We made sure that the lord had a cozy seat in his front patio. The evenings were full of music and dancing. Tom and I learned to drive a car, and Tom taught me to ride a horse, adding to everyone's entertainment because I frequently fell to the ground; it was a long training session. Tom and I enjoyed walking hand in hand in the evenings, we loved being together under the stars, and one day he asked me to marry him, and I said yes. We knew that we had to face both families, but we were strong enough to be on our own if we had to. First we let the Lord know of our plans, and he smiled and said that he was happy. When we met with the elders they let us know that, following my parents death, they had changed the rules, and as long as we were committed to the Gypsy life, that we could be wed and live as part of our family with the caravan.

Our lives were happy, I continued to work in the library, and Tom was growing vegetables in the greenhouse, and we were looking after the Lord.

One morning he called us in for breakfast together, and then he let us know that he was leaving the manor and grounds to us in his will. He had also set aside funds to secure my sister's future. Tom and I were surprised, and more than a little uncomfortable, but thanked him for his generosity.

That evening we met with the elders and let them know about the gift, we also let them know that we wouldn't know what to do with a big house, and would certainly not live in it. One elder suggested that the house and grounds around it could be given to a Trust that would run it and perhaps open it to the public. We could let him know that we would like a little more land as our caravan was growing, and when Tom and I put this to the Lord, he was very happy.

We had a beautiful wedding with everyone from the caravan, the Lord, my parents and brothers, and friends from my work in London. It was a day filled with happy moments, especially when my parents met the Lord—my dad took it easy enough, but my mum was very nervous. The party was held on the manor lawns, we had planted flowers around the trees in advance; everything was beautiful. We had a pig roast and vegetables and fruit from the greenhouse, and breads and pies baked by the ladies. My mum was fascinated by the big ovens that the ladies used outside in the caravan.

We continue with a good, happy life. The Lord passed away two years after we were married, but he was able to see our first son. We now have two boys and I am expecting our third child. I would not change one step of my life, and hope that you have enjoyed my story.

MEETING MISS JULIET

CHAPTER 1

I had just left my last surgery of the day and was looking forward to a soft comfortable chair and a smooth drink when the phone rang. I looked at it before picking up and a smile came to my face; my friend Gordon was calling. We had been friends since university in Edinburgh, where I had been taking my medical training and he was studying finance. We had passed through periods of being broke and sharing meals, to eventually finding ourselves both in good careers, often unable to get together because of the demands of our work. We were both now thirty-four and were established in our fields and lucky enough to be living and working in California.

Gordon's first words were, "I need a break, my life's been eight years of a nonstop career-building drive and I need to go somewhere where my brain is not being fried by numbers and clients; I've made so much money and haven't had a chance to enjoy any of it, any chance you could take an extended break and come with me Malcolm?" He spoke so fast and was out of breath.

My brain had been going to sleep, so I took a while to come together and comprehend his request. My schedule flew into my head, and responsibilities with regard to the various boards I was involved with, and other commitments. When Gordon spoke I knew he was serious, and he was right, we hadn't taken holidays for years, being satisfied with the odd weekend concert and trip to the theatre. So my first question was how long he intended to go. His comeback was quick, "Two months over Christmas and the New Year, when everyone is happy and celebrating, we can go five star and enjoy some skiing, fine dining, dancing, theaters, maybe a concert or two, maybe find a pretty girl to keep us company."

Over the next week I reorganized my commitments for the Christmas season, making sure I was covered for surgery hours. We were back and forth with ideas of where to go and what kind of accommodations we were looking for, deciding the five-star hotel was our best plan, somewhere near a ski hill with good food and a ballroom for the evenings. We settled on Lake Tahoe, and a five-star hotel which appeared to cover all our needs. Time went by quickly, and soon we were on our first-class flight to an unknown experience.

CHAPTER 2

Our rental vehicle was ready at the airport, and I drove to the hotel; the parking was across from the entrance and as I pulled in a large SUV taxi pulled in beside us. Stepping out onto the snow, I saw a girl open the rear of the taxi and step out in bare feet, wearing a thin summer dress. She went to her toes quickly and bounced from the cold on her feet. I quickly moved over and picked her up, she was as light as a feather. I told Gordon I would take her into the foyer and come back to help him with the luggage.

Walking briskly to the hotel, the door opened and in front of me was the registration desk, and to my right was a lounge area and a nice fire. I went over to the fire and placed the girl in a chair where she would soon warm up, but she was shaking and said her feet were freezing; she was leaning down trying to warm them with her hands. I sat on a stool and put her feet on my knees, wrapping them with my scarf; she had her head down and was holding her knees, I grabbed a blanket from the chair beside me and put it around her shoulders.

The doors opened and a young woman came in, assisted by two of the hotel staff, with a very full suitcase trolley. Beside her was a man in his thirties, who came straight toward the desk and said, "Miss Juliet's keys please." They were thrown over to him from a young man at the desk, and he walked down the hallway in front of us. The young woman looked at me and smiled, then she went to the desk and completed paperwork. The man came back and said to the young woman, "The room is safe, you can go down," coming over with what appeared to be the intent of taking the young girl. He smiled at me and said "Thank you." However, the girl put her hands around my neck and I ended up picking her up and he asked "Would you mind taking her to room one." Gordon was by this time standing at registration, and he nodded at me to go ahead. As we walked down the hallway she nuzzled into my neck and kissed me, saying "we will meet again."

I was shocked and was glad to get to her room. The double doors were opened by two of the hotel staff, and we entered a large, beautifully furnished guest suite. The young woman entered behind us and directed the suitcases to a large dressing room; the young man directed me to the large bedroom, and I placed the girl on a white four-poster bed, taking the blanket there and covering her over. At a quick glance the walls and furnishings were in white and gold with lemon carpets. There was a beautiful lit fire, lounge area, bar and kitchen.

I left, and Gordon met me at the door, he said that our suite was further along the hallway, room three, it seemed the rooms on this floor had single digit numbers; it was a beautiful suite with two bedrooms and all the comforts, including a lit fire, two large comfortable chairs, and a bar. We sat with drinks, mulling over the strange start to the holiday, then rested till dinner.

Before going to the dining room, I saw the young woman seated in the lounge and went over and introduced myself to her. Her name was Anna, she said the man with her was John, and they were travelling with Miss Juliet, then she laughed and said that was Juliet's work name. She and Juliet had been friends since childhood, and John was their driver and work friend. I made a comment, "And more than a friend," meaning that I had seen a bulk under his right shoulder, and was curious, but she just smiled.

Gordon and I were seated with two couples at dinner, it was a very entertaining time and we all planned to go skiing together the following day. Anna and John dined together; I did not see Juliet. We left the dining room and went into the ballroom, the orchestra was directly in front of us at the far end of the dance floor, we were seated around the edge at tables, halfway down on the right, and were able to watch the parties as they entered. Anna and John entered and were seated to the left of the dance floor, the bar was behind them, where half a dozen young men wandered around the bar.

I glanced over, and as the orchestra began to play, Juliet came from a side hallway on the far left on the arm of a big man dressed all in black. Juliet took my breath away—this was not a child, this was a beautiful, stunning young woman in a lemon and white ballgown which floated over her body. They stepped forward, dropping her shawl and purse on Anna's table before stepping straight to the dance floor, and without a movement out of place, they were waltzing around the floor, floating, I could not take my eyes from her as they danced one after another, laughing and smiling, I wanted her to be in my arms smiling back at me. He eventually took her to her table, kissed her on the cheeks, and then took Anna to the floor. John took Juliet, and again my eyes could look at nothing else. They all returned to the table and the tall man took Juliet in his arms and hugged and kissed her. He then left and returned along the back hallway.

Later, in our suite, Gordon and I discussed whether she was in the sex trade, maybe a high-class hooker—that was how her situation appeared—and what path had led her there. Were Anna and John in charge of her? That would explain the gun inside his coat.

CHAPTER 3

We enjoyed the following day on the ski hill, taking a long lunch with new friends, and taking in the sunshine on the slopes. As we returned to the hotel, Juliet and Anna were walking out towards the town center, so I decided to make a quick change and then head in that direction.

Eventually I saw John ahead of me, leaning against a shop wall, watching ahead of him across the road through the parking lot to the stores up above. Anna and Juliet were window shopping, but ahead of them were a group of people with cameras and what appeared to be microphones, and obviously heading in the girls' direction. I watched John who appeared ready to pounce if called, and when Anna put her hand up John was across the road and the parking lot heading up the hill where he stepped in front of Juliet and was quietly telling, what I assumed was the press, to step back before there was trouble.

I arrived shortly behind John and watched as he took hold of one photographer and asked him for his film, he said he could hand him the film or see his camera smashed to the ground. It was an intense situation, and eventually the film was handed over. No one appeared ready to move, and so John quietly opened his jacket and put his hand slowly in, at which point they were all obviously aware of what he was going to take out. He told them all to step slowly back and return to their vehicles and leave the town, and that if he saw them again the outcome would be very different.

John was ready to return to the hotel, Anna was also ready, but Juliet wanted to carry on shopping. I stepped in and offered to keep her company and, because the press had been chased away, my offer was accepted and we parted. Juliet wanted to stop for a coffee first, so we stepped into a tiny tea shop with just three tables, both enjoying the warmth of a jug of coffee, the smell of fresh baked breads, and the heat of the tea shop. I decided to gently ask about her relationship with her two companions, and she told me that she and Anna worked together, and that John was in the same business. She confirmed that she and Anna had been friends since childhood, and this was the first holiday they had taken, and they had twisted John's arm to come along with them to help with the driving, so all seemed well in that regard, though not totally clear, however I was a little relieved.

We wandered along looking in the store fronts and went into a jewelry store where Juliet found a silver locket for John's daughter, and a plaid scarf for his son. We returned to the hotel and agreed to see each other on the dance floor later. There followed five enjoyable days, skiing during the day, and dancing in the evening. I noticed that Juliet's party didn't go skiing.

On our sixth day Juliet had mentioned spending a day travelling out to Yosemite National Park, it was a long drive so we had to set out early in the morning. Gordon went to the ski hill and I joined Juliet and Anna on their trip, with John taking the wheel of our rental vehicle. The girls chattered a lot about flowers and perfumes, and I enjoyed the ride, not having to drive. It was a beautiful wilderness park with amazing waterfalls and giant sequoias. Eventually we decided to stop in the village for a late lunch, visiting a very attractive delicatessen and enjoying homemade baking and tea.

As we headed back to the car I pulled back from everyone and looked into a store window, staying there till the man behind us reached me; I stepped backwards, and faced him. He had a camera case on his shoulder and a large camera in his hand, I said, "See the man walking with the ladies, he is their bodyguard, and I can assure you he is not a person you want to tangle with." I then caught up with the group and we were not followed. When we were seeing the girls into the car John looked over at me and nodded; I felt I had received his approval.

CHAPTER 4

It was December 22nd, and I had decided to take an early swim in the hotel pool. Juliet was sitting beside the pool in a lounge chair; she was talking to someone. There was no one present, but I assumed she had earphones she was using. She was smiling, and happier than I had seen her during the whole holiday, she was looking across the water and did not look at me, she spoke about skiing and meeting at the restaurant at the top of the hill; as I had not seen her skiing, I was surprised. She then told her friend that she was returning to her suite for a while; she got up from her chair and, without appearing to notice me, she left the pool area.

That day and the following day, Juliet was very distant; she wandered around from the lounge to her suite, and went outdoors, forgetting her coat, but frequently making phone calls. John would follow her out and put a coat over her shoulders. I couldn't see the earphone beneath her hair, but she was completely distracted by the person on the phone. I noticed that John kept a distance from her, but was always aware of her.

On the second day I ventured over to Anna and sat with her beside the fire, and she apologized for Juliet's rudeness; she said it was very unusual.

Christmas Eve came, and I found Juliet at breakfast time, making use of the dining room for wrapping gifts. She was laughing with Anna, while John ate his breakfast alone. I joined John and was glad to see that the girls were back to normal and had dozens of boxes to wrap. John's wife was arriving later that day with his children, they would all have dinner together in the dining room and he asked if Gordon and I would like to join them. Everyone seemed relaxed again, enjoying the festivities. The hotel put on plates of appetizers and hot apple cider for drinks, while everyone wrapped gifts or read books in the lounge and enjoyed the Christmas noise and smells of baking. Walking past Juliet's suite, I noticed a huge Christmas tree in her lounge area, with parcels around the base and more decorations throughout the suite; she obviously loved Christmas.

Gordon and I joined their party for dinner that evening; it was a happy table; Anna was seated beside John, his wife, their son and daughter, I was next, and Juliet was seated beside me. There was a spare seat between Juliet and Anna, and a tall gentleman arrived introducing himself as Benjamin. Juliet gave the gifts to the two children, and there was much chatter and laughter as we enjoyed our dinner, along with other tables who were enjoying the festive treats. In the early evening John took his family back to Juliet's suite; Anna explained that his family was going to have their Christmas Eve together, while we retired to the dance hall.

Benjamin took Juliet out onto the dance floor, and Gordon went with Anna, so I found myself dancing with a pretty young thing whose company I enjoyed. Benjamin eventually took Juliet back to our table, and one of the single young men from the bar stepped over and sat with her when Benjamin walked into the back hallway. I took my young companion back to her table, and was able, at last, to join with Juliet and take her onto the dance floor. I cannot truly express the joy I felt when holding Juliet, my hand on her waist, her hand in mine, dancing close together, breathing in her hair, and seeing her smile up at me. I have yet to see her in the same evening dress, and today she was in a dusty pink with pearls in the top of the dress; she is perfect in my eyes.

John's wife and children stayed between Christmas and the New Year, they did go skiing as a family, while Anne and Juliet enjoyed each other's company shopping in town, or wandering into little coffee shops. They purchased exquisite gifts that encased roses and other flowers and showed them to us on our return from skiing, it became a routine to meet with then in the lounge for a drink before getting dressed for dinner. Gordon had found a young companion and would spend a good part of his evening in her company. We were both getting the rest, relaxation, and enjoyment that we were on holiday to find.

On New Year's Eve I wanted to get closer to Juliet, I had a feeling that she was going to be someone very special in my future, but in my mind was the concern for her distance created by her phone calls. I spoke with Anna, who was also concerned, and said that she would discuss it with Juliet when they returned home from their holiday. At that time I learned that they lived in Southern California.

New Year's Day changed everything; a phone message called me back to the hospital. A train derailment meant I was needed and had to take an early flight home. Gordon returned with me, and we both agreed that it had been the holiday we both needed. Before leaving, I had asked Anna if we could exchange contact information, which we did. She sent me the occasional notification that Juliet was well and back into her workaholic state, which was a very happy state for her to be in.

One day, nervous of the answer, I asked Anna what that work was, and she told me to look up "Perfect Rose." The next evening, after work, I sat down with my laptop and found Perfect Rose at Maison Banner Perfumery. The website showed acres of flowers, the majority of which were roses, and there was a factory where the perfume was manufactured. The factory was surrounded by acres of lawns, and gardens. The photos of the fields of flowers, and the factory buildings were beautiful, just like Juliet, and I spent hours re-reading about her and the company she ran, and how Perfect Rose came into being. Now I understood a little more why John was present as a guardian, although I thought the weapon was a little overboard.

CHAPTER 5

Gordon and I decided to take an extended holiday again the following Christmas, this time we coordinated with Anne for the location and found ourselves booking Colorado, with hotel and spa facilities. We arrived in the early evening, and the hotel seemed very similar to the one the previous year. Juliet and company did not arrive until the following morning, at which time we all had hugs and kisses and were in a happy state as we headed for breakfast together. I sat beside Juliet, and somewhere during breakfast I took hold of her hand and she looked up and smiled at me; my heart pounded.

There was a familiarity to the events of the following days. Gordon and I went skiing and made more friends as we lunched on the hillside and enjoyed mostly sunny days in the snow. Juliet and friends spent their day times together, and were always full of sunshine, sitting in the lounge when we returned. We had dinner in the hotel, and moved to the dance hall for the evening, I couldn't have been happier.

On the third evening, Juliet did not join us for dinner, and Anna and John were late and in a hurry. We did all go into the dance hall, and shortly I found why; Juliet arrived with Benjamin and, after dropping her scarf and purse, they went straight to the dance floor. Why was he there? what hold did he have on Juliet? my mind was black. I did not like how he held her, and when they returned to the table I boiled as he held her tight and kissed her before leaving.

Anna touched my arm and directed me to the lounge, where she stood and held her hands on either side of my face, and had such a soft smile of understanding as she walked me to the hotel registration desk, and the wall behind the desk. She pointed to the name on the wall: Benjamin Wilson. He was the owner of the Wilson chain of hotels. I looked at Anna who was smiling at me—Juliet was Benjamin's daughter. We took hands and returned to the dance hall.

We enjoyed sleigh rides and outdoor theater, went snow shoeing near the hotel where Juliet felt safest, and visited local wineries and cheese factories. My heart felt like a concert was playing everyday inside me, and one evening, after a night of dancing, I took Juliet in my arms and gently kissed her. She smiled, and we kissed again before saying goodnight.

December 22nd came and Juliet was sitting in the lounge talking to someone through her earphones, she did not look at me even though I sat right beside her, and she pulled her hand away when I tried to hold it. She stood up and walked out the door, and John followed with her coat, and managed to get her to put it on. She headed to the town with John following, and Anna came and stood at the entrance. Who was Juliet talking with? My heart sank, this person came between us again.

That day and the next I watched as Juliet walked into town and back, or stood on the fence around the sheep nearby, either talking to this person or thinking quietly to herself, and not noticing anyone around her. She did not come into the dining room, nor did she come dancing. She laughed and smiled and talked quietly with someone while sitting in the lounge by the fire; she was so happy. Benjamin came and sat beside me looking concerned. I couldn't eat, and the idea of dancing was not even a thought. I did not have to worry about Gordon; he had found a pretty girl for company and was having the holiday he wanted.

December 24th came, and along with it the smiles and laughter that I looked for with Juliet, but a little sadness in my heart. I watched her and tried to understand her. Anna said that this never happened any other time. They were wrapping up dozens of boxes of gifts, and now I realized that they were wrapping gifts for the hotel staff for Juliet's father. They knew how to make everyone happy at Christmas, the hotel was full of food, drinks, music and laughter, and the delicious smell of Christmas baking, and Juliet and her father were a big part of that.

John's family arrived, and this hotel had many more children, so we had laughter and joy as many gifts were opened. In the early evening the families returned to their suites, while we departed to the dance hall. There were smiles everywhere, the tables were full of chatter, and I was able to put my arms around Juliet and take her to the dance floor. She danced so beautifully and never stopped smiling while looking into my eyes; I could not resist her.

New Year came and I did not say the words I wanted, the feeling that her heart could be elsewhere was holding me back. My holiday was again cut short on January 2nd when I was called back to the hospital.

Anna said that she thought she knew where my feelings were going and so she had to tell me about Juliet's past. She told me about Juliet's accident, when they had been on a short holiday with her parents and her fiancé, Nigel, spending some family time together before their wedding. Juliet had been injured in an avalanche, where both her mother and her fiancé had been killed. Her father had her airlifted to a hospital in Switzerland where she spent months being treated for serious injuries and learning to walk again. The couple were both just eighteen years old, and now Juliet was twenty-three and had physically fully recovered. I thanked Anna for telling me. I was able to say goodbye to Juliet this time; we kissed and said we would keep in touch.

How could I keep this romance going, who would she meet before we could get together again, would I lose her for my hesitation? I watched her on her website as she walked through her fields of flowers and talked about her love of roses and the perfume they were making that year. She also invited people to attend her perfumery, where her staff would take them through the process . . .

CHAPTER 6

One weekend I left and went to her place of business. The drive through the fields was intoxicating, the scenery heavenly. As the Maison Banner came into view, I pulled to the side of the road and stopped the car. In front of me through the gates to the left was a large colonial house, a veranda around the front of it. Across the road were large buildings, the tallest being a bell tower. The other buildings were old and rock-built, and to the front of these buildings was a huge lawn with a large tree to the right.

As I arrived at the first building, Juliet was standing there quietly, with a sweet smile on her face, and I knew she was mine. We kissed and held each other tightly; it was so hard to let her go. We went into the factory, and Anna was there in a white robe, working with test tubes and at least eight other staff; she had a bright smile for me. Juliet talked about how they were extracting natural oils from plants and pressing and steaming them. We wandered outside again, John was talking to field hands, and he waved at us before we then drove over to Juliet's house—the colonial house—which had been beautifully upgraded. We walked in her gardens, having drinks while dinner was prepared inside. Following dinner, we sat quietly on the sofa and although it was not cold, the fire was lit.

As the evening drew to a close Juliet said that she had a secret to tell me, and she hoped I would understand. She said that we would not be able to sleep together. I was a little surprised, but waited patiently. She told me that she and her fiancé had both been eighteen, and had been waiting for their wedding day. The enormity of this grew on me, my heart throbbed, I hung my head and she held my hands gently and waited. I could hardly get the words out, as I said quietly that we could wait. We talked and planned, and spoke of seasons, and schedules. The days went by quickly, and one evening after we had been out for dinner, we walked in the rose gardens, the perfume was amazing and I felt it added to what my heart now felt it could say. I went down on one knee and asked Juliet to share her life with me, to marry me and be my wife, because I knew I would love her forever. I took the ring box from my pocket and looked into her eyes as she said yes, and I placed the ring on her finger and we kissed passionately. I went home with the knowledge that we had planned our wedding for the following spring.

We messaged frequently and during that summer Juliet made me laugh with her tales of the new hotel her father was building, the different customs and not knowing the language—he had to use an interpreter. He was stepping away from the ski hills and finding an interest in historical buildings. We were both incredibly busy, and it was Anna who suggested a Christmas holiday again. This time Juliet jumped in with the idea of going to her father's newest hotel in Croatia. Flight and passport arrangements had to be made and we looked up Croatia on the internet to learn a little more of the customs of where we were going.

CHAPTER 7

Gordon could not join us for this trip; he admitted that he had been seeing a girl from our last vacation and it was becoming serious, and so he wanted to spend this holiday with her. So, the four of us travelled together and found our way to Benjamin's new hotel. This was a very different holiday, incredible historical buildings, red rooftops, Roman ruins, a protected harbor, coastal beach land, old cobbled streets to wander in, battlements to wander over, and markets of intoxicating spices and fresh foods. We wandered for hours enjoying walking into old neighborhoods, some were rows of small houses, and toward the water were larger newer buildings. The town was filled with the beauty of history, and the waterfront was where the new growth appeared to be.

In the back of my head was the difficulty Juliet seemed to face on the anniversary of her accident, my hope was that our love would carry her over that.

The morning of the 22nd I was called to the phone and had to advise two surgeons in a complicated operation. Later, I wandered through the hotel meeting Anna and John and asked them where Juliet was. Concern came to their faces as they said that they thought she was with me. We first asked the help of the hotel staff and searched the hotel and grounds, then realized we had to look further afield and each of us took a direction through the narrow streets around the hotel. We asked for help from the hotel staff again, also reaching out to local authorities and those who knew the streets better. We could not find a trace of her, and night came when we had to stop until daylight arrived.

What happened next was relayed to me by a young man, Justin, who had been in his garden throwing balls for the dogs who lived at the house. His eye was taken by a young woman wandering along the sidewalk and seemed to be talking to herself, she wandered past him and didn't reply when he spoke to her. Something made him decide to follow her, and so, locking the dogs behind the gate, he walked swiftly to catch up with her.

He couldn't see her, but there was a park ahead and once on the corner of the park he looked over the grass to the trees, and then out to the ocean when his breath stopped as he saw that the girl had stepped over the rocks and was walking out to deeper waters. He called to her as he ran, but she did not seem to notice him, and so he ran out over the rock and into the water. When he reached her, the water was over her waist, she was still moving forward. He put his hands around her waist, but she continued to pull

against him, she was calling to someone, asking him not to go without her, he could not understand all that was said, but eventually she stopped pulling at him and she let him take her back over the rocks to the grassy area. She collapsed on the grass, and he picked her up and carried her back to the house where he was staying.

She didn't appear hurt and so he took her into his apartment and then through a connecting door to the main house, and to his right was a guest room where he lay her on the bed. Realizing that she could not stay in the wet clothes, he took pajamas from a cupboard and towels and discretely undressed her, dried her, and put her into the pajamas, then covered her with a large soft blanket. He took her clothes out of the room, hanging them on a metal coat rack that was in the family room. By this time it was evening, and he was exhausted and went to bed.

Early the following morning, Ivan, the owner of the house, entered the family room and noticed the clothes on the coat rack. He smiled to himself and wandered over to the guest room to see what his friend had done, and was shocked to see a young woman on the floor, having fallen from the bed, and half covered with the blanket; he lifted her back onto the bed, taking a gentle look at her face.

Ivan left the room and sat in a large comfy chair which was set opposite a matching large sofa, wondering what may have happened to lead to a girl in the guest room. Justin came from his rooms, sat on the family sofa, and relayed the previous evening's events to him. They heard a door open, and the girl walked out, dragging the blanket with her, and she promptly sat on the sofa and leaned against Justin.

A knock at the door found a young man standing holding out jewel-encrusted slippers and a matching purse, saying that he thought they might belong to a guest in the house. Ivan took them in and put the slippers beside the coat rack and went over to the sofa where the girl was sleeping again. He looked inside the purse and found the name Juliet Wilson, with a key to Room 1 at the new hotel. He decided to call the hotel who promptly put him through to the room where Anna answered, and after a short discussion, she said she would come promptly to the house.

Within ten minutes Anna and John entered and took charge of their young sleeping friend. Juliet opened her eyes and, looking at her friend, said "Anna, Nigel has gone, he left me on the rocks and he would not take me with him, he said that he had friends waiting and that I couldn't go with him, He told me to go back and follow my heart on a new path, he said that he wouldn't be coming back. I called to him but he turned and left me."

As she relayed this story, I had arrived, the door was open, and I stepped inside and watched and listened. I stepped over and knelt in front of Juliet, holding her hands. Her eyes were bright but she smiled at me and I just knew that all was going to be well in the future. Lifting her up, I wrapped her in the blanket and carried her out to the car, John joining me while Anna stayed behind to explain a little of the situation to the two men left behind, and stop them from calling the authorities to have the water searched for a body.

Back at the hotel we talked, the air was lighter, and my heart was lifted. I knew that Nigel had let her go so that she could be with me, and I said a prayer of thanks to him. Juliet's father stayed close with us that holiday, and when John's family arrived, I felt we were all one big happy family. Juliet went for a walk by herself one day, and returned the pajamas and blanket to the white house. She stayed for some time talking, and when leaving she invited them to our wedding in April.

There was much activity during the early part of that year, Juliet and I had to return to our professions and help with arrangements for the wedding which was to be held on the front lawn of the Maison Banner.

It was a beautiful day, there were two large tents to protect us from the sun, with just one hundred guests; we were happy to see the two Croatian young men among them. They stayed in one of the guest cottages for the following few days, and Anna enjoyed taking them on tours; it was a happy time all round. Juliet walked across the lawn to the wedding arbor, and we said our vows in front of an ordained uncle of Juliet's. The festivities were just what the doctor could have ordered, and we laughed and kissed; the day will be forever in my memory.

Juliet's father had presented us with a honeymoon, we didn't know where, just that the car was ready to take us to the airport and that all arrangements had been made. Well, we did make one detour from that, we went quietly over to Juliet's house and locked ourselves in, and I carried her to the bedroom. Our first night was to be one filled with the tender care and love that I wanted her to know from me; a night we would never forget.

The flights were rearranged the next day.

THE SCAVENGER HUNT PART 1

CHAPTER 1

Yvette was standing quietly behind the closet door thinking over how she had got herself into this fix. This dare had gone to the extreme, but she was always up for a challenge and without thinking she took it on.

She heard the key open the door and someone drop items on one of the chairs on the way to the shower, she knew there was just one man who had booked the room for a summer stay. The water was turned on, and she waited just a few moments before stepping forward and looking into the bathroom where a man was in the shower. Fortunately, the glass was glazed and so she was able to step in and reach for the bath towel, stepping backwards toward the door and standing quietly. His shower over, he reached for the towel, and not finding it, he stepped out of the shower, looking at Yvette. She couldn't resist saying, "Wow, you're pretty hot!" She handed him the towel, stepped back and ran quickly for the hall door.

She raced two doors down, having already propped the door open with a spoon on the floor, and closed it quickly, standing still and trying not to breath loudly.

She heard his door open, and his footsteps in the hallway, then he returned to his room. She waited for a few minutes until she felt all was clear, then she ran for the stairs and went down the three floors and out into the huge dining room, over to a smaller meeting room. The large round table had five people seated there and they all looked up expectantly when Yvette entered, laughing with tears in her eyes. They all did high fives and congratulated her on completing the challenge.

Yvette asked, "Have we received the first location for the scavenger hunt yet? I think maybe I need to get out of the hotel for a while," her face still full of tears of laughter. Yvette and her five friends were on this holiday seeking adventure, and they had added an element of challenges. All aged between twenty-one and twenty-six, they were immensely intelligent and were at the start of their promising careers, but they were nonetheless good, kind and honest people.

Yvette had finished both school and university at the age of sixteen and found it difficult to fit in to her own age group. The friends had met in Matthew and Yvette's parent's house in Oxford, with Colin and Janet video calling, and Johnathan and Caroline staying over with them for the weekend. They were discussing holidays, and how bored they were, not wanting beaches or skiing; how they wanted to try something exciting to get through the holidays. Matthew's father suggested that they find a really well-travelled friend to create a scavenger hunt for them, using the three weeks that they were all going to be together; knowing they had few concerns about the expense of traveling. Colin's father owned an international company, and was thrilled to take up the challenge of creating a scavenger hunt.

The holiday came and they packed for all situations, water, snow, rock climbing, and decided to leave bags at home with extras, should they be needed. They all met at Matthew and Yvette's father's hotel in California and, while waiting for the first clue, they came up with the idea for creating small challenges for each other, and they each wrote a challenge on a piece of paper to keep themselves occupied in the hotel, placing them in a jar. Yvette was the first one to take the challenge, and was happily successful.

The man from the shower had come down and was standing looking at Yvette sitting at the table; she stood up and went back to the window in the room, her friends stepping around to protect her; the man smiled at her and walked away.

CHAPTER 2

The fax machine started shooting out pages—the first clue from Colin's father. It was easy for all of them to know that "Milkweed and Dense Clusters" meant the Monarch Butterfly, and it was the right time of year to visit Mexico, but what would they find there? Deciding to take the climbing gear, they all returned to their rooms to pack. As Yvette walked to the elevators her friends joined together behind her, letting her go up alone, because they had noticed that someone was waiting for her and they blocked his way. He said to them "Would you mind telling that young lady that my name is Liam Campbell and I would like a few minutes of her time to talk."

Matthew had been busy on the phone arranging flights to Mexico, and watched Liam move away to the lounge. He found it easy to make the bookings, being the slow season, and arranged for a van to take them all to the airport. As they all came down the elevator, they were met by hotel staff who took some of their cases and put them into storage. Liam was watching this and so he knew that they would be returning. When they left he spoke to the boy who stored the cases and was told that, as far as he knew, they were a group of students on a scavenger hunt.

Liam had not intended getting involved with a female on this trip; he was busy doing research on some new programs he wanted to promote at the university, his days were busy commuting from one research facility to another and having considerable studying to do in the evenings.

The friends had the maps out on the plane and were discussing how to get around, whether to take buses or rent a vehicle, and with all their heavy gear they decided a vehicle would be best. Once off the plane and into their vehicle they headed out following the maps, and had fun negotiating the rocky roads, taking them close to two hours of driving. Once they were closer to the sanctuary they had to change to horses, carefully packing only what they needed around them on the saddles. They went very slowly as they were surrounded by millions of butterflies, and eventually stepped down from the horses and tied them to a tree. They used binoculars to view the walls and trees where the butterflies were dense.

Johnathan moved some distance away and started to climb the shorter wall. Once on top, looking down, he was able to look along the wall into the crevices and, after a two-hour search he said, "I've found it." Now, how to get to it, first it was at the highest part of the wall and there were people around who would not like him climbing over butterflies, and second, he couldn't tell how large it was, and how far it was pushed into the crevice. There was a tree nearby and he called down and asked if anyone could swing from the branches to reach the crevice. Janet was the smallest of the group, so they threw a rope over a branch and she was able to climb up to the first branch. She climbed higher and then tied a rope to the branch above her, swinging and stretching her legs out to the wall, eventually touching the white item and causing it to fall to the ground.

They all scurried around, and Matthew opened the paper wrapper; inside was a knife, and on the paper was written, "Return this knife to whence it came to complete your challenge."

They took the horses back to their vehicle, then sat in the parking lot studying the knife, looking for any markings that would lead them to its original location. Janet thought that she had seen something like it in the museum a few blocks away from the hotel they had been staying in, so the decision was made to return to the hotel and search from there.

Returning to their hotel late that evening, their bags had all been returned to their rooms, and having had very little sleep, they all took time to rest.

Yvette had ordered a light supper to be delivered to her room and she went in for a shower. As the trolley was being delivered, Liam stepped over and told the server that he had left his key inside; giving him a tip, he took the trolley and went into the room. Yvette called out that the tip was on the table beside the door, so Liam then closed the door. He walked quietly over to the shower and slipped into the room; taking the towel from its peg, he waited. He had a cheeky smile on his face as she stepped out of the shower and realized what had happened, and he stepped forward, but instead of handing the towel over, he wrapped her in it and stood holding her, looking into her eyes. He then picked her up and carried her into the room and placed her down on the bed, when she realized his intention. Now she was afraid and started to fight. He was surprised and, looking into her face, he saw tears in her eyes. He sat up and said, "I'm sorry, I thought that was what you wanted," and standing, he then left the room.

Yvette went down to the lounge looking for her brother Matthew, and she found him beside the shrubbery near the elevators. She was trying to explain what had happened, but she was stumbling over her words. Liam had stepped off the elevator and stayed close by where he could hear what Yvette was saying. Matthew had realized what had happened and he was saying to his sister, "You knew something like this could happen Sis, you and your silly challenges, remember what you have is special, you can only give it once, so make sure you give it to someone you really care about, we can only protect you so far." She was snuffling and he continued to hug her and took her into the bar for a drink.

The next day Yvette let the others search the museums while she stayed in her room. They were lucky and by lunchtime had located the correct museum with the empty knife slot. They found their own way to unlock the case and return the knife to its rightful place without being discovered, before heading back to the round table to celebrate. They were all looking at the challenge jar, and Janet was brave enough to take a turn. She left them and went to the drugstore to buy a huge sketch pad. Returning to her room and looking in the papers for a picture of the mayor, she started sketching a caricature of him with huge nose and ears and long Medusa hair. Once the sketch was done she took out earrings and put them in his ears and nose, making a very grotesque picture. In the evening she asked Colin to go with her, and she pasted the picture on the front doors of the City Hall. The next day the picture was front page in the newspaper.

CHAPTER 3

The following morning they were all having breakfast when the fax machine started up again. This time it was "If you take this piece of paper away it will fall over," and of course they quickly guessed the Leaning Tower of Pisa, what would they find there? They couldn't decide what equipment they would require, so they packed as tourists. Again, their spare bags and equipment were stored for them. Matthew was again booking tickets, finding that the earliest flight would be the next afternoon; he sent a text message informing all of them of the change and telling them to store their bags safely.

Most of them were either in or near the meeting room and Colin said that, as he had a clear day, he would take one of the challenges out of the jar. He opened it up and said "Oh no, this is not for me, if I were to do this I would get killed, certainly not me." He looked around and seeing Yvette he said, "You're the only one that can do this without getting killed." Yvette took the paper and, after reading it, she put her hand with the note into the air, striding to the doors with a huge grin on her face. She got into the first taxi and headed away.

Liam asked Matthew if he could speak with him; they sat in the lounge and Liam explained what had happened with Yvette, and that he truly thought what had happened was what Yvette had been wanting. He said he would never seduce a person as it looked, he wanted to explain that to Yvette, and try to get to know her. Matthew guessed that was what had happened but he said he didn't know how to help him, he didn't want to get involved with his sister's crazy schemes; also, he said that his sister was no fool, both he and his sister had graduated university before they were sixteen, and although she was very smart in one way, she had put up many barriers to deal with her lack of age and experience.

While they were talking they saw Yvette return, she walked slowly in and spoke to one of the staff and he walked over to the open door to the manager's office and looked in, returning to her and speaking quietly. Yvette walked past the reception and turned quickly into the office and was gone less than a minute before she returned and walked into their meeting room.

The manager returned, and within ten minutes there was a roar from the office, "YVETTE! WHAT HAVE YOU DONE NOW!" and it sounded like a chair crashing over and the manager came stomping out of his office holding a water glass in front of him, heading to the meeting room. Those staying at the hotel and sitting close by were intrigued. Yvette got up from her chair and raced over to the window looking back at her father with her hands over her face trying to cover up the fact that she was laughing. He stood at the end of the table and thumped the glass down and pointed at her then at the glass, yelling, "YOU DID THIS, YOU PUT TADPOLES IN MY DRINKING WATER, WHAT AM I TO DO WITH YOU!" He continued to point first at Yvette and then at the glass, then sharply turned and stomped back to his office, making sure that the door was closed before he smiled and shook his head. Yvette quickly ran to the doors and went outside to walk it off; she couldn't stop laughing.

Matthew turned to Liam saying "Are you sure you want to get to know her, do you see what you would be getting yourself into. It's my job to keep her safe from herself sometimes." Liam just looked at the spot where she had left the hotel, amazed.

Following breakfast the next morning, they had all moved their bags to the entry. Liam came over to Yvette and tried to speak with her but she stepped backwards and, walking past everyone, she was the first into the van.

They had a first-class flight, enjoying the special amenities served to them, and on arrival they decided to take a taxi to their destination. Standing away from the Leaning Tower, they all speculated on what they would find; they walked around viewing all angles yet could find nothing out of the ordinary. Colin suggested they climb the stairs, all three hundred, and as they went slowly upward they searched the walls, the window slots, and the steps, but nothing stood out and they were being watched by some curios tourists. Caroline was the last one down the steps and she kept a distance between herself and the person in front, when she noticed a tiny white spot sticking out of the lower step. She showed it to the others and they all gathered around, trying not to be too obvious.

Colin tripped and fell right beside the step with his hand over his head, and while the others gathered to help him, keeping other tourists away, he put his hand under the step and took an envelope that had been stuck there with gum. They walked away and stood discussing the location and discovered that it could not be seen going up the steps nor on the way down, except for that half inch of white. They congratulated Caroline on her sharp eyes.

Once seated comfortably inside a coffee shop they opened the envelope to see a flat piece of very old paper with what appeared to be a recipe, like an old family recipe. Now they knew that once again they had to discover where it came from and return it without being discovered. They were speculating whether all of the items they were finding came from somewhere near the hotel, and whether Yvette's father was somehow involved, however on return to the hotel he denied having anything to do with it.

The recipe was Italian, and there were many Italian restaurants to cover near the hotel, and they decided to separate into couples, pretending to be celebrating their engagements as they attended each restaurant; asking whether there was some famous family recipe that was a specialty. They found there were many family recipes, and slowly they returned to those restaurants, carefully asking what was in certain dishes; fortunately, they all enjoyed the food they were tasting. They read over the items on the list for the recipe and were eventually able to work out which restaurant they needed, and spent some time talking with the owner, and following a number of drinks, they learned that the recipe was kept in a safe in the office. Locks were not a problem for them; they entered the restaurant that night, and Caroline was able to unlock the safe; there was no recipe inside, and so they returned the one they had to the safe.

The following day, after a celebration breakfast, Caroline decided it was her turn to take a challenge and took a folded paper from the glass bowl. She smiled and said, "This one is easy for me," and returned to her room to change her clothes. Caroline was tall and beautiful, all the men would turn and watch her, and she had dressed specifically for this purpose, with a low-cut neckline and bare midriff.

She took a taxi to the Police HQ and entered the building, keeping her eyes open for signs, heading to the chief of police's office. All heads turned and followed her, no one asked her where she was going, even the women looked, wondering who she was, and nobody noticed that she was carrying an empty shopping bag. She tapped on the door and entered the chief's office with a smile, she was glad that he was in uniform, and behind Caroline was a sergeant who came in to pass the chief a message. Caroline quickly placed her shopping bag near the table where the chief's hat was, and pushed it into her bag. She moved to the door and said, "I can see you are busy, I will come back later," and she walked quickly out of the building. Returning to the meeting room she tossed the hat on the table saying, "One challenge down," and smiled.

They were two weeks into their holiday and the chatter around the table helped them understand how much they were enjoying their time together, and Yvette found that, although they were all older than her, they were all good friends.

CHAPTER 4

They were looking forward to the next challenge arriving, and while they were eating dinner the fax started to shoot out pages. "Water, 1 of 4, Barefoot, Feed the Birds," were the clues that came with it. Well, Colin said, "Feed the birds would take us to London for the movie Mary Poppins, but what does that have to do with the other clues?" They lazed around occasionally thinking of the clue, finally deciding to sleep on it.

Liam had been sitting near and listened to the clue, and he knew the answer, but was not going to say anything. The next morning he was in the breakfast room early and waiting for the young people to come down. The place was buzzing with chatter from the meeting room, and when Matthew came down he said "I've got it, the four things to do with water are bridges, and there are four bridges going over the Grand Canal in Venice, I just don't get the Feed the Birds clue?" Liam smiled.

They all decided to take the chance and head out without completely understanding the last part of the clue. Once again Matthew was in charge of transport details, this time he also booked a hotel for a night. What to take: underwater gear, water resistant clothing, and someone suggested appetites for good food. Now they wished they had more time to travel to Venice, taking cruises and train or coach tours; next year they would have to take more time for a visit to Venice, they all agreed.

Once again, they had a comfortable flight, and on arrival decided to take a taxi to their hotel, hoping it would be for just one night, and once settled in they set out on a walking tour, followed by a gondola ride under the bridges. The lights at night were quite beautiful and they understood how romantic Venice was.

The next day, splitting into two groups, they decided to enjoy more gondola rides while viewing the underside of the bridges. Meeting for lunch, no one had found anything unusual that attracted their attention.

Following lunch, they again decided to break into two groups and start walking over and around the bridges, keeping in mind to look for something to do with birds. Yvette, Colin and Johnathan spent a few hours going around two of the bridges and came up blank, they were sitting on a park bench waiting for the other group to contact them. Matthew, Caroline and Janet had searched the first of their bridges and had moved over to the second bridge. They had started at one end and went slowly searching crevices, and anywhere that something could be hidden.

Matthew stood up straight, stretching his arms into the air to take the strain off his back, when he noticed balloons at the end of the bridge; he called to the other two to join him. They walked to the end of the bridge where an elderly lady was sitting on a chair to the side of the bridge, holding the balloons. Matthew looked at her and said, "Feed the birds," and she smiled at him. She asked him whether it was the "barefoot" clue that made it too easy for him, and he had to admit that he had omitted that clue. The lady laughed, telling him that it would have led him straight to the Scalzi bridge. She pointed under her chair and there was a large box for him to take away.

He sent a message to the others to meet back at the hotel, and there they opened the box, with looks of surprise on all their faces. There was a college mascot in the box, a wolf in parts! How would they get it through customs and return it to the correct college? They put the box in a suitcase in a cupboard, and, as they had arranged to stay a second night, they headed out for dinner and a final gondola ride.

They were all up very early for their flight the next morning, and because the mascot was in three pieces, it was shared between suitcases, with a simple crossing of fingers.

No one questioned them as their suitcases were placed on the belt, nor on their return; luck was with them, and their suitcases were not opened. With a large sigh of relief, they found a taxi and returned to the hotel.

Yvette's father was at the reception desk when they arrived, he looked at them, giving a long stare at Yvette, and said, "No more mischief." They all returned the parts of the mascot to the box which they placed in Matthew's room, and again took time to settle in and rest from their eventful journey.

It was easy to locate the correct college, now how to return the mascot to the college, knowing that students were returning and they were all over campus.

Caroline decided to take a tour of the college. Carrying books in her hands, she set out wandering in and out the different hallways, heading to the lower floors, and again to the upper levels as far as she could go. Back outside again, on the lawns she saw a sign saying "Student Guide" and she stood beside it hoping someone would come. It was only a few minutes before a young man in student colours came forward and offered his services with a huge smile. Caroline thought he was cute and was able to ask a number of questions and, finding him with quick answers, she asked him whether the college had a mascot. He said he would take her to see it, but she quickly declined, saying she had an appointment to get to, but asked where it was located so that she could go there another day. He happily told her that the mascot was in the basement, in a cupboard where the Sports Hall of Fame was located, and was locked for safety.

Caroline returned to the meeting room triumphant, now they had to decide how to return the mascot to its rightful place. There didn't seem to be much point in planning to enter at nighttime because these days, before college started, the campus seemed to be alive twenty-four seven. They had to go downstairs to the Sports Hall of Fame and place it in a cupboard there. They watched the campus, and the delivery trucks, and how the delivery men were dressed, and decided that would probably be their best access., but how to get into the room with the Sports Hall of Fame, because it was locked and they didn't know whether there was a special combination.

Liam had left a letter in Yvette's slot asking her to meet him. He was in the bar, hoping that she would be more comfortable at a table beside the wall than sitting out in the lounge. She arrived ten minutes late and, looking for him, moved through the tables to where he was sitting; she sat down nervously. He asked her what she would like to drink, the waitress took the order, and he thanked her for coming. He said, "Please don't run away, let me speak and explain that I had no intention in harming you, it was just that your move and the words you spoke in my shower room gave me the impression that you were playing a game and seeking more attention, I honestly didn't understand what happened when I was in your room, I had no intention of doing anything against your will."

The drinks were delivered and Yvette picked up her glass and kept it close to her face, looking at him. Finally she spoke, saying, "I realize now that it was a prank that got out of hand, I should have known what might have been the consequences and I am sorry for having used you in such a way." Liam looked at her and asked her if all was forgiven, and she said yes, and hoped he forgave her for the prank played upon him. He said that it had never happened to him before, and he smiled, making Yvette blush. Liam asked if he could take her to dinner one evening, however she told him that their vacation was coming to an end and she was returning to England with her brother. They had a couple of things to do before leaving and she did not have enough time. He tried to arrange a lunch meeting, however she refused and said she was sorry that she had to leave and returned to her room.

The friends met in Matthew's room and Colin offered to be the delivery man, locating the building where the vans were kept, and easily found a uniform to fit him.

The following day they waited for the delivery truck to appear. Parking behind it, taking out a trolley from their own vehicle and moving the mascot box, they headed into the building. No one questioned Colin, and Johnathan was wearing the college scarf from a peg in the hallway, and he stayed close to Colin, making sure he was able to negotiate the stairs down to the correct room. Colin was relieved to find it was a regular lock, and while Johnathan stood to block him from the view of students, he was able to get into the room. He stood carefully to one side of the glass door, protected by a wall, and watched the students as they went by. Johnathan leaned against the door, also blocking the view as much as he could. Colin slid the box across the floor, and quickly stepped over to open the door of the cupboard, only to find that the lock needed a key. He went over to the desk and started opening the drawers, then, looking round the walls he found the key on a peg beside a picture. Quickly unlocking the cupboard, he placed the box inside, locked it again and put the key back on the peg. He stood stiff on the spot as someone was talking to Johnathan, and when she moved away he raced for the door with the trolley and quickly stepped outside.

Walking happily together out of the college they placed the trolley back in the trunk of their car. Colin removed his coveralls and hat and tossed them in the back of the truck. Back to the hotel, and into the meeting room everyone was there waiting for them; a huge cheer went up as they did a thumbs up with happy smiles. After dinner they all sat in the lounge with drinks. Liam took his drink and sat close to Yvette; she gave him an annoyed look.

CHAPTER 5

Johnathan decided it was time he took a turn at the jar of challenges. Taking a piece of paper out, he opened it up and smiled. "Just up my alley," he said. He went off with a taxi driver he had asked to take him to charity stores, asking the driver to wait while he went inside, and then moved on to the next one before returning to the hotel. Just shortly after midnight he headed out, borrowing one of the cars

from the hotel, which he knew were there for the group's use. He went to a number of the charity stores and let himself in, knowing how to manipulate the simple locks, and came away with boxes of shoes and runners, remembering to leave payment for them beside the tills.

He drove over to the seniors' residence center and parked to the side, climbed over the back fence and came back with a tall ladder from the work shed. Placing the ladder beside the huge tree that was in the front lawn, he started at the top of the tree and carefully hung the shoes close together from the top all the way down to the bottom, then he placed the remaining shoes in the boxes and closed them up and placed them under the tree.

The next morning found some of the residents sitting on chairs outside having their morning tea and enjoying their *shoe tree*. The press, being previously warned with a special request to make this an amazing day, had arrived to interview the residents, carrying supplies of coffee, tea, and boxes of treats, which Johnathan was sure would make their day and give them something to talk about with anyone who visited.

CHAPTER 6

They were all together having a final dinner the night before their departures when Colin's father walked in and joined them. They all cheered, and there was a lot of loud chatter and laughter among them and it was a very happy evening.

Johnathan wanted to know how he had been able to make sure no one else took the treasures. Colin's father told him that for the knife he had had to use a cherry picker in the middle of the night to secure it in the wall, and normal people would not climb the wall and it could only be seen from the top. The envelope at the Leaning Tower was placed there, again at night time, and if they had noticed a man all in leathers and chains standing close to the steps, he was there to protect it, and because he was rather scary looking, people moved away from the lower steps quickly so no one else found it. The mascot was easy; a friend in Venice was delighted to take part in the little game and was glad that it did not rain while she was sitting there as they had taken longer than expected to find her.

Johnathan asked Colin's father how he had been able to get hold of the items found at each location and he tapped the side of his nose saying, "That's my secret," and smiled.

Liam decided to take one last try at gaining some future contact with Yvette when they were all signing out at reception. He did know that Yvette and her brother were heading back to England, and their friends were all heading to different destinations. He stepped beside her and asked her where she was completing her schooling, and she looked at him wide eyed, then smiled and told him the university she was returning to, and that she was returning to her position as senior tutor while furthering her studies, and that her brother was in charge of his own research department at the same university.

Liam smiled at her saying, "In that case I will see you both on opening day, I am the new associate dean."

THE SCAVENGER HUNT PART 2

CHAPTER 1

It was the first day and all students were in the auditorium and staff were sitting on the stage. The dean was welcoming students returning and new students attending their first year, then, after introducing their new associate dean, Liam Campbell walked out onto the stage. Yvette kept her head down and blushed. When everyone was dismissed, Yvette headed directly to her office, sitting down and wondering how she would cope with the new associate dean.

Liam looked around and could not see Yvette in the auditorium; he wondered how he would handle their first meeting. Yvette was happily back with her students for three days a week, and for two days she was studying for her master's. Her days were busy and she enjoyed the laughter in the classrooms.

A week into classes she received a note from the associate dean requesting that she attend his office the following morning before class. She had a struggle sleeping that night, and was bleary-eyed in the morning, using a little makeup to cover it up. Entering Liam's office, he didn't look up but asked her to take a seat. Feeling ready, he lifted his head and looked into Yvette's face and thanked her for coming at such an early hour; he could see from her eyes that she had had a stressful night.

Liam said that this was just a get-to-know-you meeting; he knew that she was teaching as well as studying for her master's and he asked her if there was anything she needed to make her situation any easier. She said that she felt comfortable with the hours that she could spend with her studies, that she loved teaching the students, and for her it was not difficult. He noted from her file that she already had four bachelor's degrees and was continuing with an interest in teaching. He didn't want to hold her up and so he thanked her for coming and, as she was leaving, he asked her whether she would like to go for coffee one day; she nodded, then left.

Rather than calling him into his office, Liam decided to walk over to Matthew's research center, and was impressed with the set up in the center and the two staff who were very attentive. They greeted each other with friendly handshakes, and Liam also listened as Matthew described where he was in his research, and with what steps he was hoping to move forward. He had taught graduate classes for a period, and when he received his grant he opened up the center. They agreed to have a coffee one evening.

Liam met Yvette at the coffee shop, and they sat for a short while, but Liam found that Yvette was nervous and so he suggested they go outside for a walk. There was a small park nearby with flower gardens and they were distracted by the gardeners cleaning out the dead plants and preparing for fall planting. He tried to take Yvette's hand, but she bunched her fingers together and pulled away; Liam was concerned with how closed she was.

He walked her back to her rooms; when outside her door he took her hand in his, it was again bunched, and he held it with both his hands, saying, "I know that when you were younger you had to put up a wall to protect yourself, but you have made a wall too deep and too high, and now it's getting in the way of you experiencing life except in a game. You were a child when you erected the wall, but you are not a child anymore, and you have to find a way of taking it down or you will miss out on so much." He walked away, hoping that she had listened.

A few days later, Liam joined Yvette at a lunch table outside, and when she went to leave he asked her to stay for a few minutes. Liam then told Yvette that he too had graduated from university when he was fifteen, and he was twelve years older than Yvette, from a time when students were more accepting. However, his life had been one of study, something he loved, and yes, he had a number of diplomas and certificates on his wall, but that his greatest achievement for him personally was a website he had put together for students with exceptional IQ's, to help them maneuver through the trials that faced them in their younger years. He suggested that she look into the website and see if it interested her.

Yvette did look into the website, seeing that it would have been a great help when she was in her early teens, when she was an outsider both with students of her own age as well as students she was studying with. She read into it further and found there might be help in dealing with her wall, which she knew was causing her difficulties when faced with challenges in the staff rooms, not knowing how to reply to some questions. She made contact with a counselor by email, and set up a Saturday for them to get together.

Yvette went to the counselor's office, which was more like a small comfortable lounge with a large fireplace and older comfortable chairs. They sat together beside the fire, and the counselor started by asking simple questions, and using the answers as points of discussion. The counselor said that she had enjoyed their first session and that she would have liked to carry on longer, but unfortunately she had another person to see, so they set up another time to meet.

Yvette returned to her suite and looked in the mirror. "How can you have such a head full of knowledge, but not know how to communicate with people," she said to herself. She knew that where she felt safe was with her brother and the friends they had made over the last few years. Johnathan had become a friend because she had been in class a few years prior and was happily answering questions that the instructor was asking, when he told her to let others have a chance to reply. She always felt awkward with both instructors and students and put her head down into her book. The older student sitting beside her said, "If anyone else could answer, shouldn't they put up their hand in order to do so," at which point the instructor moved on with the class.

Johnathan met with Yvette outside, and she thanked him for speaking up. He told her to try and stay a little quieter in class, he knew that she knew the answers, but sometimes it was best not to let everyone know how smart you were. He asked her how many degrees she had, and when she replied that at that time she had three, he whistled, and smiling, he said, "Yes, I see your problem, just sit with me when we have the same class and you should be OK." She couldn't understand why she needed his help, but they found themselves in a routine of sitting beside each other, and later she found that he was a friend of her brothers. When Matthew learned of the closeness between Johnathan and his sister, he went in search of Johnathan, who made it clear that she was only like a sister to him; he just felt that she needed someone watching over her, and so all was well between the two friends.

CHAPTER 2

Liam spoke with the counselor and asked if there was anything he could do to help Yvette. She advised "We cannot discuss her case specifically, but by creating a wall people miss childhood, teen years, and companionship, if you are interested, try to fill in the gaps."

Liam went away thinking of his teen years and what had filled his days. He pulled out photo albums and found what he needed. He went into his storage cupboard looking for any items that he had kept from his camping days, most items were still there. Pulling them out he put them on his bed to see whether they were still in good condition, and found most in order, just a few things would need to be replaced—after all, it was ten years since he had last gone camping.

Now, where to take her, one night away and somewhere not too far so that they could spend an evening and a full day, returning late on the second evening. Campfires, hot dogs, s'mores, English muffins with sausage rounds and cheese, macaroni cheese, fresh fruit. Now, how to get her to feel enthusiastic about such a trip, and not be afraid. He invited her over for coffee after supper one evening and directed the chatter to his years growing up, knowing that this was awkward for her but trying to direct her to his photo albums. He kept talking while turning pages, saying how much he missed that time in his life. She said that she had not been camping but it did look as though he and his friends were having fun. He made his move by saying, "I don't have friends to go with anymore, do you think you could come and keep me company, we would eat over a camp fire, and take walks in the woods, it is very peaceful and quiet in the woods, we would take two tents and sleeping bags with extra pillows and foamies to lay on." Yvette had been trying so hard to take down the wall that she had put in place in her teens, and with this in mind she agreed to go.

They ended up going to a private campsite where Liam knew the managers, because he realized she would not be comfortable without washroom facilities. He had set up the two tents in among the trees with Yvette's help, and they both put in their bedding. Sitting beside the fire they enjoyed hot chocolate and s'mores, telling each other the fun things that had been happening in class, which also showed Liam what a great teacher she was. He put out the fire, saying it's time to sleep, and said goodnight, watching Yvette to her tent.

He had been listening for some time at the noises of the forest, being at peace and remembering the many evenings he had camped, when he heard something and saw Yvette crawling into his tent. He stayed still and she moved up close to him and laid down, not moving. He asked her what she was doing, and she said a bear was coming into her tent and she was afraid. He suggested he take her back as there were no bears in this park, but she insisted on not moving. It was too cold for her to lay on the ground as she was and he suggested she climb into his sleeping bag, making very clear that he was in his pajamas and she was also in hers. As usual she was very trusting and climbed in and leaned over him for warmth. He lay there knowing that this was going to be a long night, and placing his arm around her he tried to rest.

In the morning when Yvette woke up, Liam was not there; looking out of the tent she found him making coffee and getting ready to make breakfast. She hopped out feeling quite refreshed, and suggested they take an early morning walk. Liam said they should eat breakfast first, then he would put out the fire, so they ate sausage and cheese in English muffins with their coffee, and once everything was cleaned up and they were dressed, they headed out.

The campsite where they were staying backed onto a small forest, and they walked together enjoying the sun coming through the trees, and the fresh air making them feel so alive. Liam took hold of Yvette's hand, and she did not pull away. They sat on a log and Liam used a piece of wood to move the moss and cleared away the soil from the log, showing her the bugs that were beneath, and later he moved the earth on the ground to show her the creatures that were surviving there; she was happy and he felt her joy.

They returned to the tents in the early afternoon and made hot dogs and macaroni, resting for an hour before getting up and packing away all the gear into Liam's truck. Making sure the fire was out and the campsite was clear, they headed back toward the university. Liam thanked Yvette for keeping him company, saying she had taken him back down memory lane. She smiled, telling him that it would be a new memory to hold on to for her.

Yvette was happy to see the counselor the following week, and told her about the camping trip and how it made her feel, the counselor was amazed at their sleeping arrangements, and thought about the strength it took for Liam to be with her. Gold star to Liam.

CHAPTER 3

Yvette and Liam had attended a lecture at the city library, and on their way home they had stopped for dinner at a small restaurant. Back in Liam's vehicle they were travelling along the city road when they both heard the squeal of brakes, and the sound of rubber being shredded on the road, there was a junction up ahead and they had time to slow, however the car in front didn't, and the SUV came spinning into the intersection and hit the car on the driver's door, forcing them both to spin and stop as they hit the posts at the side of the road.

Yvette was out of the door before Liam's vehicle stopped. Racing over with her phone out dialing for emergency services, she looked at the driver of the car and could see that he was trapped inside. She touched his shoulder and said "I'll be back," and she ran over to the other vehicle where it appeared to her that the driver had been killed.

She returned to the car and helped the female passenger from the front seat, taking her over to the sidewalk where there was a bench for her to sit down. She was bleeding heavily from a gash on the left side of her head and face. Liam had also called for emergency services and was helping the other three passengers from the SUV. One was able to walk and helped with the other two passengers. Liam had his first aid kit from his car, he knew that one of the passengers had broken bones in his leg, but he was helping as much as he could to control bleeding while waiting for the ambulance.

Yvette had returned to the car driver and was gently rubbing his shoulder and held her hand on his chest where she could feel his heart pounding. She spoke softly to him, encouraging him that help was on the way and she would stay with him until they arrived, she continued to talk gently to him and to encourage him to stay calm. It wasn't long before they were surrounded with ambulance staff and emergency services assessing the situation. Liam helped get the people on the sidewalk into the ambulances, and Yvette had been asked to stay where she was until they were ready with the jaws of life. She continued to soothe the driver of the car until she was thanked and asked to give her name and phone number before leaving. She went back to Liam's truck where he was waiting for her.

He drove Yvette back to her rooms—by this time she was shaking—and escorted her up the stairs and went in and looked for her drinks cabinet, which Yvette said she didn't have. She did have bottles of wine and a bottle of sherry and he poured her a drink. He sat beside her on the sofa, she said that she just wanted to go to bed, and standing up she went into the bathroom. She returned in pajamas and, climbing into her bed, she asked Liam if he would stay till she fell asleep. Liam sat in the chair beside the bed and marvelled at how he could sit there with her looking as beautiful as she was.

Liam was talking with Yvette's counselor over the progress that was taking place. Yvette was taking control faster than expected, and it was good to see her moving and speaking with confidence. The counselor said that she would not be seeing Yvette anymore, unless Yvette requested a meeting.

One evening while walking in the park, Liam moved Yvette backwards against a huge tree, then took her hands and put them above her head, and looking into her eyes he told her that he was falling in love with her. She looked at him and said, "What does falling in love mean?" Taking her arms down, he leaned his back against the tree beside her, and moving his arm around her shoulders he pulled her in close to him. He tried to explain to her that, for him, it meant when he knew in his heart that he always wanted that person to be in his life, to share his feelings and plans, "to be mine," and for her to want to feel the same way.

It was close to Christmas and Yvette wanted to do something special for her students and she arranged to take them to a pantomime. It was across the city so they would need to travel on a student bus, and because the boarding school was already closed for the holiday, she arranged for them to all have dorms there. They were playing *Aladdin* this year and she felt sure they would enjoy it. She asked Liam if he would assist her, and if they could use a school bus. Liam wondered where the financing for the tickets came from, then reminded himself that Yvette was financially secure and was using her own funds.

The event turned out to be a great success and Yvette had loaded the dorms with junk food for them to eat and drink until it was lights out and the men went to one dorm and the girls to the other. Liam smiled at these arrangements.

Yvette asked Liam if he would like to join her family for Christmas, however he was going home to spend the time with his mother. Yvette and Matthew travelled to the family home and their father flew in from his hotel in California. He had arranged for a friend at a local hotel to deliver their Christmas dinner, and with the table set and the room filled with the delicious smells of the Christmas baking, they all sat down. Yvette's father made a toast to the empty seat, saying words of love as they remembered their mother who had died when Yvette was in her early teens, leaving her father and Matthew to raise her. Her father was able to lead them all in cheerful festivities, the dinner was amazing, and they loved being together for the holiday. Just a short piece of family business was to decide whether to keep the family home, and they all agreed that they did not want it sold.

On their return to the university both Yvette and Liam found themselves with heavy workloads, yet they would make time late in the evenings to get together over a drink or coffee, usually in Yvette's rooms, and they both enjoyed this time of getting to know each other. Sometimes Yvette would experiment making a cake or muffins, she had not had a mother to teach her, and many of her experiments were without recipes, so Liam enjoyed trying the results and planned for them to spend a lot of time together in the kitchen. Sometimes she would also talk about her studies for her master's, and these times he enjoyed getting to see what was circulating inside her.

CHAPTER 4

Liam wanted to take Yvette somewhere special, and he thought that she might like to go to London for the weekend to see a theater show. He was able to purchase tickets to *The Lion King*, which he had not seen, and he found that Yvette had not seen either. They both enjoyed the performance and Liam had booked a late dinner for them at the hotel they were staying in.

Following dinner, they had drinks in the lounge and were comfortable with each other, talking about the many things that they had in common and what achievements they were both seeking for their futures.

Liam told Yvette that he had booked one room for them in the hotel. He watched her reaction, and she asked to see the room. They went to the elevator and travelled up in silence. Liam took her hand on leaving the elevator and they walked down to the room, he opened the door and she entered, walking over to the window. She looked around the room and said "I've forgotten my overnight bag, it's still in your car."

It was here that Liam wanted to know her feelings, and he turned to face her and said "I am yours, are you mine?" He left to get the bags from the vehicle, and when he returned to the room he saw her at the window facing him and she said, "You are mine, yes, I am yours," at which point he dropped the bags and stepped forward, taking her close in his arms.

GRANDMOTHER'S WISH

CHAPTER 1

Monica was busy packing her clothes into a wheeled suitcase, preparing an overnight bag for short stays, getting ready to take a holiday with her grandmother. She had listened during family conversations, with her grandmother saying that she would like to take an extended trip to visit places that were special in her heart and see old friends, knowing she would not be returning. Monica was coming up to her first break from college courses and wanted to enjoy that time with her grandmother, so she offered to accompany her on the holiday. Her grandma was so excited, and plans were set in motion. There was a certain amount of preparation because passports were needed, as well as permits necessary for crossing borders.

They were both living in Croydon, and the day came when Monica loaded her bags into her car, then locked her apartment door and spoke to the landlord before leaving. She drove over to Grandma Diane's apartment to load her suitcase and get her settled in the front seat, with a blanket wrapped around her. Then they made a quick stop at a coffee shop to pick up a coffee and a tea, before hitting the road.

Avoiding cities where possible, they headed to the underpass between Dover and Calais. It was a cool start to the morning; they stopped in Dover for a croissant and hot drink before heading to the underpass. Diane kept her head down and eyes closed going through the underpass, she really didn't like it, but once in France she was fine.

Driving along the beach front in Calais, the views were of beautiful sandy beaches. It was a bright day, with clear blue sky and wispy clouds. They parked the car to look across the Strait of Dover to the white cliffs, rising over three hundred feet out of the water. They had booked a bed and breakfast for that night, and went and checked in and were happy to see they fronted the water, with seats outside for evening relaxation. Monica asked for a good place to go for dinner, and following directions, they headed out

and found a beautiful historical seafood restaurant with an amazing menu where they enjoyed sea scallops with steak and potatoes with a glass of wine. It was a restful evening, chatting while their meal was prepared and relaxing in each other's company. Returning to the bed and breakfast, Monica asked for extra blankets to use outdoors, and they sat looking out over the water until the evening got too chilly, at which point they moved inside and had hot milk together before going to bed.

In the morning they had a lovely breakfast prepared for them of orange juice and coffee, with croissants, poached eggs, bacon and a selection of cheeses. They then headed out to the hotel where they were meeting other companions for the guided coach trip they were taking through Europe, where Monica left her car in secure storage.

With suitcases loaded they all boarded the coach, finding themselves with very comfortable and spacious seating, and settled in. The first part of their journey took them along the coastline to Amsterdam, with wonderful coastal views and a very knowledgeable tour guide to entertain them. When in Amsterdam they enjoyed a canal cruise. The canals were very busy, and after stopping for something to eat and drink they went on to visit the Amsterdam Museum, a magnificent museum, again with a very knowledgeable guide. The night was spent in Amsterdam with good accommodation, and they breakfasted with other travellers before heading out to the coach and moving on to the Rhine Valley.

The coach took them to their riverboat cruise, their guide telling them stories about the castles that they saw on their way. From there they followed on to Innsbruck and continued on to Munich where they were given a guided tour throughout the city, taking in a traditional beer hall before dinner. Their accommodation throughout the journey was exceptional.

The following day they arrived in Florence and had time to walk about and enjoy lunch. The next stop was Venice.

The coach was braking as it headed down a steep hill, the driver becoming aware of a cement truck attempting to pass at a great speed. There was traffic coming uphill toward the coach and the truck did not have enough time to complete the pass and he pushed the coach over to the side, where the soft earth gave way, and the coach careened over the embankment into open air; it rolled over, travelling down the embankment before landing upside down. The noise of the metal crashing against rock and the screaming by the passengers was deafening.

Many vehicles up above stopped and their occupants raced to the aide of the injured, some making phone calls for ambulances and fire and rescue. It was a steep hillside and there was great difficulty in getting any mobile passengers up to the road. Many of the injured were helped out and were sitting on the rocks, or laying on the ground, with good Samaritans helping them until the ambulances arrived. Some passengers were trapped in the bus and there were people sitting with them comforting them, others appeared to have died of their injuries. Everyone was eventually taken to a local hospital to be identified and have their families contacted.

Monica's Aunt Roberta was phoned, being the person who had been left as emergency contact, and was given the sad news that her mother had died in the crash, and that Monica was very seriously injured. They gave her details, saying that they would keep her up to date following Monica's return from the operating theatre, although they warned that she had been in a very serious condition. There was so much activity taking place at the hospital, firstly to care for those who had been injured and who needed special care. Those who had died in the accident were taken to the morgue and would be taken care of later.

CHAPTER 2

Diane had always had a strong faith, and Diane's soul had left her when she died at the crash site; moving toward the stars and the higher heavens, her soul was met by others who were to prepare her for her journey; she felt at peace. Words were not spoken, but a knowledge of thoughts and feelings—an understanding—passed between each soul and Diane realized that they were waiting for Monica to join them, so that she could travel with her.

Diane's soul became very agitated and the other souls could feel her unrest and could see the picture passing through her mind and heart of how wonderfully Monica had cared for her parents during their illness, and to the very end, and then how she had taken over caring for her grandmother, returning to her home as often as she could during college to care for her needs. Monica had not had a young person's life; she had not gone to parties, or even had a boyfriend, she had so much in her heart to give. The souls could sense the strength of these feelings, and a soft blue light shone gently forth from them, and what followed was the most incredible pure white light shining all around them, and Diane found herself having left the others and was travelling through the stars to the high heavens, amazed at the feeling of peace and contentment she had, that she could carry on alone.

Monica was taken from the operating theatre to intensive care, and was attached to many tubes and pieces of machinery. She had been there two hours when her heart failed, and the hospital staff rushed in a defibrillation machine and, following three attempts with the paddles, she was returned to life; however, she was in the hospital a considerable time before her aunt was notified that she was able to travel back to England.

Monica's grandmother had been buried before Monica returned to England, and after some time Monica was told that her grandmother had left her considerable estate to her. She found that in the paperwork was a letter from her grandmother who hoped that she could continue to enjoy travelling, and that one day perhaps she might fall in love.

Monica had not been able to work following the accident, but when she was able to walk and move about without discomfort, she decided to return to the accident site, and continue from there on the journey that she and her grandmother had planned. As all the paperwork and her personal papers had been destroyed in the accident, she went through the process of renewing everything before she could set a day to travel.

Two months later she flew to Venice and was greeted by a cheerful guide who drove her over to the hotel where her journey would begin. She booked into the hotel, meeting other guests who were going to be taking the same coach tour. She had spoken with the guide and he had offered to take her to the accident site; later that afternoon they drove out and parked safely so that Monica could walk to see where they had left the road. It was a sad occasion, however she spoke to her grandmother and let her know how much she missed her, and she hoped that by completing this journey her grandmother would be at peace.

They spent a few days in Venice, with an excellent guide who took them to see so many beautiful pieces of artwork. Venice is a very romantic city and he took them to see the Rialto Bridge, the oldest bridge over the Grand Canal, built as a pontoon bridge in 1200, and rebuilt many times since then.

They travelled next to the Bridge of Sighs, which was built of limestone, and had walls with windows to view from. The bridge connected to the Doge's Palace where prisoners went for interrogation. The palace was built in 1340, and in 1923 became a museum.

In the evening they headed to the gondola pier in the center of Venice, and were entertained on a magical tour while being serenaded, ending the evening by finding a restful place to enjoy a late dinner.

CHAPTER 3

The following day they headed to Trieste where they had time for a walking tour, and a stop for lunch. Their following stop in Pula, Croatia, was the final destination for Monica; she was to be staying with Mr and Mrs Novak in their boarding house. Her grandmother had been friends with Mrs Novak, who was overjoyed at her arrival, greeting her like a daughter with many hugs before showing her to her room. It was a joy for both of them to talk about Monica's grandmother, to learn more about her from each other.

After a few days, Monica felt that she knew her way around enough that she left the house one morning and went for a leisurely walk to the park, enjoying the early sunshine and the quiet of the morning. She had been sitting down for quite some time resting on a park bench when she decided it was time to head back for her breakfast; however, when she stood up she caught her handbag strap on the arm of the bench, and turning to release it she stepped backwards as she pulled, unfortunately falling right into the path of a jogger who knocked into her, sending her down backwards on to the grass with him falling down on top of her, getting his hands to the ground in time to stop himself from crushing her.

Without thinking she said, "You are very beautiful," and he gazed at her before getting himself quickly to his feet and putting his hands out to help her up. They both spoke at the same time, apologizing for their part in the fall. Then there was quiet and he offered to take her for a coffee. She quickly said thank you but that she had to deal with her coat which was a pretty pink that now had grass and dirt marks on it, and she turned and quickly walked to her residence. He watched her as she walked away, realizing he didn't have her name, and then turned to continue his run.

Monica was enjoying walking the network of cobbled streets in the neighborhood and learning to speak a little of the Croatian language. She also enjoyed being a tourist heading out to the many battlements with views out to the breathtaking sparkling blue seas. She enjoyed walking alone and was not afraid to find new places to search.

Mrs Novak sat with Monica at breakfast one morning, telling her that she and her husband were attending a music concert in Zagreb the following Monday, and wondered whether Monica would like to join them. It would mean staying in Zagreb overnight; they would arrange for a suite for them all, returning the next day. Monica was so excited, of course she would love to go, and asked what form of dress it would be. This was going to be an occasion where she could go to town with an evening dress; it was going to be so much fun.

Monday came and, with overnight bags packed, she joined Mr and Mrs Novak at their SUV and when comfortably seated they headed out to Zagreb. It was a beautiful drive, and to Monica the scenery was always amazing. They booked into the hotel and were shown to their suite, which was beautifully furnished, having a connecting door to another bedroom for Monica; she was overjoyed with the comforts provided there.

Dressed for the concert, they stopped for a drink in the lounge before being called to their taxi outside. As they went through the doors, she saw the young man she had fallen in the park with, who was entering the hotel; he gave her a surprised smile.

The concert began and the musician who entered was none other than the man from the park. Monica had tears in her eyes for most of the performance, she felt her heart and soul being filled with the music, frequently having to remind herself to breathe; it was a breathless night to remember.

Following the concert they decided to have a final drink in the lounge before heading to their suite. Conversation was pretty happy among all the people in the lounge who had been to the concert, when in through the doors came Stavisa, the musician. He took Monica's breath away as she lowered her head, and was surprised when he stopped and spoke to her saying, "Its nice to see you again," putting his hand out and taking hers. He had hoped that, like most girls, she would say her name, but she stayed quiet, not looking directly into his face. He turned to Mr Novak and they shook hands, as he did with Mrs Novak, then he asked them their names and where they came from, thanking them for coming to see his show—now he knew how to trace where the young girl was staying.

He looked at Monica and winked, as if to say "if you won't give me your name, I have other ways." He ordered drinks for them all and sat in a lounge chair with them, joining in the friendly chatter.

It had been a wonderful evening, however Mr Novak felt that Monica looked tired, knowing that she was still in recovery from the accident, and he suggested they retire for the evening. Stavisa took Monica's hand and slowly kissed it, making her heart race and making her blush considerably. As they left Stavisa thought to himself, *one challenge down,* and smiled.

Two days later beautiful flowers arrived for the "ladies of the house," bringing knowing smiles to Mrs Novak. By this time Monica had learned a few things about Stavisa, one being that he was quite a ladies' man, and was the life of parties. Monica had grown up in a very gentle environment, not attending parties or flirting with young men, so she felt it wise to stay away from him.

One morning he phoned the house and spoke with Mrs Novak, who said that Monica was out on her morning walk, and so thanking her, he set the phone down knowing he would be going out the following day.

He stood in the trees in the park the following morning and watched where she would cross the road and enter the park; he felt his heart racing as he waited, and felt the heat of a smile inside when he saw her. He waited until she was just out of sight, and decided it was time to catch up with her. However, she was not so receptive to his greeting, saying, "Thank you for the beautiful flowers, Mrs Novak really appreciated them," as she carried on walking. He tried to encourage her in conversation when she said, "If you don't mind I really appreciate my quiet morning walks before breakfast, it helps me to think better during the day."

Well that was a good brush off, Stavisa thought, and he nodded and jogged ahead. *One down to her,* he thought, but he was not giving up.

On the morning of the community market Stavisa walked into the back garden over to the dog playpen and picked two of the small dogs out, setting them on the grass while he fitted jewel collars on them, and then added rainbow leads for each of them. They were happily bouncing around him as he headed to the market. He had a bag for picking up fruit and vegetables and he had his list from his chef. So many people knew his little dogs and were stopping to speak with him that he didn't notice Monica walk up beside him until the dogs bounced around her, getting the leads trapped round her legs.

She stood still, looked down and, with a huge smile, picked up one of the dogs, nuzzling into it saying, "Looks like you are a very spoiled little man." She then turned and faced Stavisa. Surprised, she stepped backwards, almost falling over from the other lead wrapped around her legs. He put out his hand to steady her and asked her to wait while he released the other dog and picked it up. She really didn't know quite what to do so she fussed over both dogs, who were absolutely adorable. Stavisa told her that he had four other little dogs and that she was welcome to come over any time to see them, he then asked her if she was shopping for the family kitchen, to which she nodded. He noted that it was pretty hard to get words out of her.

She didn't object as he walked along with her. Taking time selecting fruit and vegetables to take home, she noticed that he really was taking quite a large bag home. They were going in opposite directions when leaving the market, so they said a friendly goodbye.

CHAPTER 4

Time had arrived for Monica to return to London but she really didn't want to go, finding that there was no one close for her to go back to. She talked frequently with Mrs Novak about her plans for returning to university, and from there her plans for her future. Mrs Novak suggested that, if she didn't want to return to London, she could stay in Pula with them and stay as long as she wanted until she was ready for another stage in her life or a plan to move on in her travels. She could look into transferring her university program to Pula or another university close by and see what was offered to encourage her to stay. Monica spoke English, Spanish and Italian, and was already able to have a conversation in Croatian; she would need to improve a little more before attending the university, however her Italian would help her.

Monica decided that it was time to take her future into her hands and telephoned the university before heading there for an interview. She was pleased to learn that her qualifications from the university in London meant that she could join her courses at more than the halfway point, and only had a year to complete her oceanography degree and to follow on with her master's. They continued to discuss where her career would lead her when she had completed university; there were many areas of ocean studies to continue in Pula and surrounding areas.

As she left the university, exploring the grounds, she again ran into Stavisa, and asked, "Are you following me?" to which he smiled, telling her that he was putting a concert together at the university and asked if she would attend. She agreed. He then admitted that he had learned she had arrived for a holiday and that time had passed, and yet she was still in Pula, and asked if she intended to stay much longer. Slowly he was able to get her to talk about her visit, the change of plans, not returning to England, and from there they talked about her attending the university and perhaps looking to continue her studies somewhere in Croatia afterwards. He walked her back to her home and gave her a friendly hug.

He felt it was time to introduce her to the people in his circle and so after arranging a party he dropped by one evening to invite Monica to his house. There was music, dancing, and his chef was planning to create many mouthwatering treats for everyone to try. He said that he came by to make sure that she would come. She looked at Mrs Novak who nodded her consent that she would be safe to go.

The evening came and a car arrived to take her to the party; she was greeted at the door by other friendly guests who made her feel very welcome, handing her champagne and showing her the beautifully decorated dance/family room and the lounge area and bar where tables were set out with the chefs specialties.

It was early evening and she enjoyed looking out of the huge windows on to a pool and lawn area. She wandered to the side windows to see a young man running and playing with some small dogs; she looked for a door to go outside with them. When outside the young man told her that he was staying in a guest suite in the house. He was not too into parties, however he had to attend as it was good networking for him and his career as a drummer. They ran around with the dogs, throwing balls and ropes, and were laughing together and enjoyed each other's company. She walked with him to return the dogs to their play pen, then entered the dance room via his suite. Stavisa watched them walk in and wondered why she arrived via the suite, when the young drummer walked by and said, "Don't worry, not my type, too sweet for me," and grinned. Monica found herself with some charming dance partners and was thoroughly enjoying herself.

Stavisa circled through his guests a few times, finally deciding that he had spoken to everyone at least once, except his special guest; he finally was able to go in search of her, finding her yet again being entertained by his young drummer friend.

He joined them and they talked together for a while until the young man left them and they were at last alone. He asked if she would like a tour of the house; he had only built it a few years earlier and was still completing the design of some rooms and finding appropriate furnishings. They were relaxed and friendly together and she enjoyed their discussion of comparisons of housing and furnishings between England and Croatia, the necessities for a musician to have a soundproof room for his home practicing, and especially for his drummer friend.

They were returning to the other guests when he turned to her and said, "So you think I'm beautiful do you," and looking slowly down at her he brushed his lips softly against hers, they stood with their eyes locked into each other for a while before stepping apart and moving into the dance room. They stayed on the dance floor, with Monica resting her head on his shoulder and him holding her close. Some of the guests were noticing the move and were wondering who the new young interest was in Stavisa's arms.

The evening came to an end and Monica's driver came to take her to the car, Stavisa having to stay and see his many guests depart, and Monica went home to her bed and slept with wandering dreams.

Stavisa had a difficult night, his insides were burning with passion for her and he was finding it difficult to control his thoughts as they rushed through his busy mind. Being annoyed with himself for having so little control, he decided again to go for a run and clear his head, sorting out why he had so much interest in her when she had nothing to do with his world of music or his life in Croatia and his travelling the world with his music; she did not fit.

He and his camera crew were set for a week away in various locations and were going to be moving fast from one venue to another. They were a fun crew and were having a huge amount of laughter from the jokes that were being told, and once at their motels they were at the bar for a good part of the evening, and later playing cards. One of the camera crew asked him who the new girl was at his last party, and normally he would say, "Just someone I picked up in the market," but he had difficulty saying those words and looked at his friend without making a reply; he didn't know what to say. They all laughed loudly and said, "You've got it bad," and he just shrugged his shoulders, he didn't know what to think but he retired early; he started to feel that this was no longer a game. He would seek out Monica because he enjoyed her company and the challenge of their conversation; they argued over many subjects but they were not angry with each other. He was no longer playing a game and it made him feel uneasy.

On their return from the tour, Stavisa found that Monica was attending the university in the daytime, and he was busy coordinating their next tour. She was enjoying going out with a couple of girls that she had made friends with; occasionally going to the bar where there was live entertainment, "If you don't understand the words of the songs you can enjoy the music" she told him, and she enjoyed the music.

His parents were having a family party at their home, and he asked if he could bring a friend along with him. His parents were always happy to have new faces come into their home, all he had to do was ask her. He met Monica after university one afternoon to walk her home, and casually asked whether she had been into many other Croatian family homes, and she had to admit that she had not. He told her about the family party at his parents' house, emphasizing that it would be very casual, and that perhaps she would find it refreshing to be with his family and four young children. She thought about it and agreed that she might enjoy the change of company, so he arranged to pick her up on the Sunday for the short drive.

Her little bit of knowledge of the Croatian tongue helped her through the afternoon and evening; she enjoyed going into the kitchen with Stavisa's mother, learning to help prepare the meal; very different to her English menu. The family had a small acreage, with two large dogs, and they all went outside to toss sticks for the dogs, walking around the vegetable gardens. Stavisa walked holding Monica's hand, and she did not seem to object—*one step further*!

When returning to her home in the car he leaned over and kissed her on her lips, then he stepped out of the car and opened her door, and putting his hands on either side of her face he said, "There is something very special about you, you make me feel special," then he smiled and said goodnight.

Monica went to bed with many questions fluttering through her mind, and butterflies in her stomach. She again thought about his reputation, but she had not seen him behave at any time in a poor way toward his female visitors and he had been genuinely loving towards his mother, and certainly was always kind toward her.

Monica was very busy with her schooling, studying well into the evenings, and so on weekends he would make a point of finding somewhere new to take her, whether to markets, climbing up to battlements, or travelling out to other communities. She seemed to love where ever he took her and he liked to take along a picnic basket for them to have at their varied destinations. They spent enjoyable weeks getting to know each other.

CHAPTER 5

Stavisa told her that he had a special surprise planned for her for the following Saturday and so she was excited to see him. He took her for a drive deep into the woods where she loved to be and parked the car. They walked in through the trees, deeper into the park where there was a pretty bridge over a stream. They were on the bridge, it was a quiet day and they were alone when he knelt down to propose to her, she was so happy that he loved her so much, but how could she tell him her feelings. She asked him to stand up, at which point he looked very sad. Monica told him how much she loved him and wanted to be with him, but that they could not marry; he was Catholic and she would not change her religion; she knew that he had been married previously. She said that she would live with him, have children with him, spend the rest of her life with him, but could not marry him. He knew that he wanted more, he had lived in such relationships, and that was not what he wanted, he wanted commitment.

They stood leaning into each other's bodies, their heads together, thinking. Stavisa began to smile and said, "Would you be willing to write vows, we both write vows, and say them to each other in public, in front of family and friends, where we can make our commitment to each other." Monica smiled and said "Yes," and Stavisa placed the beautiful antique ring on her finger and kissed her passionately.

Mrs Novak took Monica shopping for a dress that floated over her body down to mid-calf, and two weeks later they met in Stavisa's garden looking out to sea. Mr and Mrs Novak were there, and Stavisa's parents and family, and all the little dogs. Monica had invited her two girlfriends, and Stavisa invited a number of friends, those that he had known from his youth, and those who were close to him in his music business.

They spoke their vows under an archway that Stavisa had created, and as they kissed everyone cheered and clapped with joy. There was a table laid out with beautiful treats and various drinks for the guests, and the happy couple enjoyed everyone's company until it was time for them to leave. They travelled to Dubrovnik for their honeymoon and their passion for each other lit sparks in their honeymoon suite with the rose hearts and champagne. It was a wonderful time for them both.

Just a few weeks after their honeymoon Monica found herself expecting a child and they were both overjoyed. Monica had time to complete her final year at university, and Stavisa made sure that he did not have any concerts at the time of the expected arrival of their baby. Time went by fast and a beautiful daughter arrived, and as she grew Stavisa loved to have her crawling on their bed and cuddling between them. He could not have wanted more, yet a year later Monica was pregnant with their second child, and nine months later an adorable little boy came into their lives; Stavisa said his world was complete. They loved taking the children to the park, and playing in the sand on the beach, making hearts and bridges, and paddling in the water, choosing a simple life at home so that Stavisa rested between concerts. Monica had her university degree and would return to work when the children were at school; she was more than content enough to spend her days making her family happy.

CHAPTER 6

Following the birth of their son Monica had to visit the specialist frequently in relation to injuries from the accident. Her heart had been weakened, and she took time to rest when the children had their afternoon naps. Stavisa did not learn of this until he came home early from a trip, when the concert had been cancelled due to flooding. It took him some time to control his feelings. He joined Monica at her next visit to the specialist and learned how weak Monica was, and for the first time he felt fear for their futures.

Monica was not really surprised, she had received a second chance at life, to share such a perfect love with someone, to bring beautiful children into the world, she had been filled with love and joy. However, she was concerned for Stavisa and was searching for someone special for him. God knew that Monica would soon be joining Him, and He was concerned that she was losing her faith, trying to make plans for Stavisa which He had already set in motion. As time went by, Stavisa would sit at the top of the bed with his legs either side of her with Monica laying against his chest, and he would sing softly to her, his breath on her neck giving her comfort. With his heart breaking, he lifted the children on to the sides of the bed so that Monica could see them and they could give her hugs.

He protected the children as much as he could during the final weeks, and he had asked Mr and Mrs Novak whether they would be willing to give up their boarding house to join him in his home; to become the grandparents on behalf of Monica to the children, to care for them now and in the future when he was away at concerts. Mrs Novak was thrilled, but Mr Novak was not sure until Stavisa said that, if he wanted, his gardener would really appreciate some help—he only worked two days a week and it was a large garden. They had agreed and were living in the suite at the house, and, with the housekeeper and chef, it made a happy home when Stavisa was away, and the children were loved and secure.

Nine months after Stavisa said goodbye to Monica, he met a young woman backstage at one of his concerts; she was also a musician and they found they had a lot in common to talk about. He eventually invited her to his home, and she was good with the children and laughed with the antics of the little dogs. As they got more comfortable with each other she told him that she loved her career and had decided not to have children so that she could continue to gain greater experience. Over the months they grew closer to each other and talked of marriage. She said that marriage was not out of her plans, but she wanted her career as well, yet Stavisa saw that she had a beautiful way with the children and knew that he was content not to have more children. Their love for each other grew and a year later he asked her to marry him. The children were thrilled and Mr and Mrs Novak were very happy to continue as they were with the family and children.

They were married in the Croatia Catholic Church and they were happy; their family life was one filled with music and laughter, fun events with everyone involved, and they had a wonderful long life together.

Stavisa would lounge beside the pool some evenings and he would talk to Monica about the children, solving problems, or laughing over some crazy things they had done, and he would always end by saying, "I will always love you."

Acknowledgments

The Tellwell organization,
for being so much fun to work with,
for helping me every step of the way,
for making me feel important,
even though I am a small cog in a big wheel.

My brother Roger Watts for being the first to read the
stories,
and keeping me sane,
believing in the way I received them.

The Ballantyne girls and their families, for all their
support and help,
without which I would have fallen on my face.

To my dear friend, for contacting me to renew
acquaintances,
suggesting how I move forward,
and giving me the title for the book.

About the Author

My name is June Ballantyne (nee Watts). I grew up with my five brothers and loving parents in the small village of Salford, Oxfordshire, England. It was a beautiful, safe, secure place to start life where we were able to cross fields and walk in the copse, enjoying the bluebells and cowslips. I moved to London when I completed college, meeting my husband there. We eventually moved to Scotland and from there we emigrated to Canada, in the Vancouver area at first. It was a busy life then, with a new family, working at City Halls, and eventually we moved to Vernon, BC. My husband returned to Scotland.

I now have an incredibly happy life with my three daughters and their families. I think my greatest gift is to see those I love happy, and for my girls to pass on the joy of life to their children. At age seventy-two, I now love to watch and listen to classical music, which takes up a good part of my morning, and I feel blessed to have such singers and musicians to keep me upbeat. I can also drive a short distance to the beach where I read and people-watch, ending my visit with a short walk along the sand. The gift of these stories will always amaze me, I just hope I have used them for the purpose they were sent for, and that is to put a smile on your face and give you a good feeling.

Manufactured by Amazon.ca
Bolton, ON

20921854R00097